Transcribed from his audio diary by Diane Ralph, with the additions found on t̲ʰ̲ ̲h̲ʲ̲ ̲i̲P̲ ̲d̲ ̲ ̲w̲h̲ᵉ̲n̲ ̲s̲h̲ᵉ died in Tuscan

1

How Babe was brought up ... a small ... ... how he came to be ejected from it.

There lived in Notting Hill in London, in the town house belonging to Sir Digby Thunder-Smith, Bart., an adopted son endowed by nature with the gentlest of manners. His appearance betokened his character. He combined a robust common sense with a simple good nature: this the reason, no doubt, for his being called Babe. Those friends of the family who thought themselves in the know believed him to be the offspring of Sir Digby's sister and of a local stockbroker whom she had refused to marry because he could not envisage getting hitched other than in their local church, a horribly plain Victorian building devoid of character or atmosphere. And he wore socks with sandals.

Sir Digby was one of the most influential of the Notting Hill set, his home being equipped with forty security cameras inside and out and no windows. His lounge was easily converted into a fifty-seater cinema, and the smallish garden was put down half to cannabis plants and half to health-giving rocket. His two-afternoons-a-week lady gardener could also supply other stimulating natural products of more potent sorts upon demand. Although officially a Catholic, Sir Digby enjoyed a very close relationship with the local Anglican vicar, who entertained aspirations to become the first female Bishop of London.

Everyone called him 'mate' and everyone was careful not to displease him.

Lady Petal, his wife, weighed a scary forty-seven kilos and earned thereby a very great deal of admiration. Her rocket-and-cannabis suppers were keenly attended. Their daughter, Madonna-Jo, was sixteen, rosy-cheeked, tall and shapely. The boy, Babe, seemed to be in every way worthy of his adoptive father, who had engaged for him a live-in tutor, giving to the local authority the justification that education by a child's parents was far superior to anything a school could offer. (Moreover, an unfortunate misunderstanding over postcodes had meant that Babe was one of the 331 applicants who failed to gain a place at the local Academy.) The tutor, Fabio Lamode, had ended up positively ruling the home, and young Babe attended to his lessons with all the willingness associated with one of his age and character.

In addition to the 'core curriculum', Mr Lamode enthusiastically taught Dawkins-Darwin Theory, Global Thermo-Dynamics, Ethnic Diversity and the Oliver Diet. He demonstrated that mankind was following an inexorable evolution towards perfection, that this progress was most aptly reflected in the pages of *Vogue* magazine, and that Sir Digby and Lady Petal's house came closest to epitomising the brilliance of that progress.

'It is quite clear,' he would say, 'that things cannot be other than as depicted in the *Sunday Thunder* 'Living' section, because we are taught there what is needed to make life good, and once these necessities are acquired we can know that life *will* be good. Eyes have evolved to receive tinted contact lenses: therefore, we have tinted contact lenses to match our lipstick. Feet have clearly evolved to be encased in Adinike trainers, and so websites supply us with those trainers. Notting Hill stands out above Shepherds Bush and Holland Park so that houses

2

BABE, or PROGRESS

Voltaire's *Candide, ou l'Optimisme*
translated into the present day

by

Keith Rumsey

Book Guild Publishing
Sussex, England

First published in Great Britain in 2014 by
The Book Guild Ltd
The Werks
45 Church Road
Hove, BN3 2BE

Typesetting in Sabon by
Nat-Type, Cheshire

Printed and bound in Great Britain by
CPI Group (UK) Ltd, Croydon, CR0 4YY

A catalogue record for this book is available from
The British Library.

ISBN 978 1 909716 05 6

like your father's can be seen to their best advantage: the house of the most progressive man in the city must be visible to those trying to keep up with him, and so it is. Asparagus evolves in all parts of the world to be eaten, and so all the year round we eat it: those who say there is a season to everything are just talking nonsense. The progressive is always in season.'

Babe would listen carefully and believe all he was told, if only because he thought Madonna-Jo had evolved to be the perfection of prettiness, though he could do no more than dream of plucking up the courage to tell her so. He thought that, if the greatest possible happiness available were to be able to live as Sir Digby, then the second greatest was to be Madonna-Jo, the third to be able to see her every day, and the fourth to be able to hear the wisdom of Mr Lamode, the greatest philosopher of Notting Hill and, therefore, of the world.

It so happened one day that Madonna-Jo, whiling away time as, with the curiosity natural to a teenage girl, she liked to do, by accessing the house's security screens on her mobile device, noticed Mr Lamode in the garden in the company of the Columbian girl who was the part-time gardener. It became clear that he was desirous of helping her to a clearer understanding of the anatomical differences that have evolved between peoples of different races and continents. Madonna-Jo, ever thirsty for knowledge – as was, evidently, the gardener – watched entranced the repeated and varied demonstrations on view. She gained a clear picture of the tutor's anatomy and of how it interacted with the ethnic characteristics of the girl. She found herself agitated and thoughtful, intrigued to know whether Babe's anatomy would interact similarly with her own characteristics.

She sent a blushing picture of herself to Babe's mobile, causing Babe to blush too. She called him up and greeted him in a rather breathless voice, and Babe replied without any very clear idea of what he was saying. The next evening after dinner, as they left the dining-room, Madonna-Jo and Babe found themselves together behind the David Hockney-inspired ornamental screen. Madonna-Jo showed Babe another picture she had taken on her mobile and Babe showed her his. Babe found himself kissing her fingers with quite unwonted tenderness; their lips met, their eyes sparkled, their legs trembled, their hands strayed. Unexpected activity causing the screen to topple, they became visible to Sir Digby who, witnessing their attempts at experimental physiology, chased Babe from the house with applications of his Adinikes to the boy's backside. Madonna-Jo fainted: her mother waited only for her to revive before slapping her cheeks. It was rather like Victorian times in this the trendiest of all houses.

2

What happened to Babe when he fell in with the gang.

Hurled thus from his worldly paradise, Babe walked for a long time without direction, tears streaming down his face, constantly turning to look back in the direction of the trendiest of all houses where lived that most beautiful of young people. Eventually he lay down to rest in the littered space between two lock-up garages. Polystyrene cartons whirled in the wind around him. The next morning, chilled and filthy, penniless and dispirited, he dragged his feet in the direction of the West End. He stopped miserably in front of a pub.

Two men wearing glasses nearly as dark as their skin noticed him.

'Cuz,' said the one to the other, 'that looks a likely lad; he looks a tough one.' They approached Babe and very politely invited him to eat with them.

'Boys,' said Babe with genial humility, 'I'd love to, but I am totally skint.'

'No probs!' said one of the men. 'Someone of your looks and build shouldn't never have to pay for nothing: your biceps must be all of forty-five centimetres.'

'Spot on,' said Babe, flexing the relevant muscle.

'Come in and sit down: not only will we pay for your meal, but we shall never allow you to want for any necessity. We should all look out for one another.'

'You are right,' said Babe. 'That's what Mr Lamode always impressed upon me; that's what we've evolved to do.'

They pressed cash and other substances on him and encouraged him to put them to immediate use.

'Who is it you see when you close your eyes?'

'Ah, my lovely Madonna-Jo,' replied Babe.

'Not her,' said one of the men. 'We expect you to see Rasta Joe, the God of Hackney, our leader.'

'Never heard of him,' said Babe.

'What? And he's the trendiest of men. You should raise a glass to him.'

'Oh, I'll do that.' And Babe did so with a will.

'You needn't drink any more,' they said. 'We look upon you now as the support, the shield, the defender, and the hero of the Hackney Family. You are assured of wealth and respect.'

Without further ado they bound him hand and foot and took him in a van to an empty warehouse. There he was taught to use a knuckle-duster and a chain, to resist tear-gas and water-cannon; he was made to learn the chants; he was given thirty lashes of the whip. The next day he performed a little better and received only twenty lashes. The day after that only ten were needed and his fellows regarded him as something of a prodigy.

Babe, stupefied, still couldn't work out quite what was happening to him. One day he took it into his head to go walkabout, just setting out and walking along, seeing the world as going past him rather than as him going through the world. He hadn't gone six blocks when four lads caught up with him and carried him off to be locked up in a small cellar. They offered him a choice: to receive thirty-six lashes from each member of the gang, or to receive twelve bullets simultaneously in the skull. It was in vain that he remonstrated that neither was a healthy option; he was required to make the choice. Using that power which has evolved in humans to determine our own destinies, he opted for the lashes. He achieved six passes through the gang, which was made up of one hundred and twenty men and girls; that made seven hundred and twenty lashes which tore every scrap of flesh from his torso. Before they could set him off on the seventh pass, Babe decided enough was enough and asked for the bullets to the skull. This favour was granted, and they blindfolded him and forced him to kneel up. Rasta Joe, happening to come in at this moment, asked what had been Babe's crime. Understanding from what he was told that the young scholar was somewhat lacking in street wisdom, this practical genius of the streets pardoned him with a show of mercy which will be celebrated down the ages in the pages of Facebook and Twitter. A magic lotion, procured online, healed Babe within three weeks. He already had a certain amount of skin and was able to walk when Rasta Joe decided to go head-to-head with the Tottenham Boys.

3

*How Babe fled from the Hackney Family and
what became of him.*

It is impossible to imagine anything more elegant, better
presented, more co-ordinated in dress and action, than the
two gangs. The chants, the rattling of the chains, the
whistles, the slapping of the leathers, the thumps of the
kerb-stones landing, all produced a harmony beyond
anything ever heard in a Punk Rock concert. First the
kerb-stones accounted for twenty souls on each side; then
the chains did for another thirty quite unable to keep up
with the trends; finally the knives removed from
circulation several score more. Babe, trembling as only a
scholar can, concealed himself as best he could from the
worst effects of this barbarity.

Eventually, while the two leaders were leading the
remains of their troops in consoling spirituals, he took the
decision to seek elsewhere the means of reconciling what
he had just witnessed with the dicta of *Vogue*. Skirting his
way around the groaning bodies he came to a shopping
mall, still burning. It had been associated with middle-
class consumerism and its contents had been consumed by
the Hackney Family according to the laws of democratic
self-interest. Here shoppers tried to assist their wives and
children as they bled from wounds sustained from the
flying glass; there girls, cut after having succumbed to the
imperious demands of the warriors to satisfy their

naturally evolved desires, sobbed for their lost beauty; others, screaming from burns, begged for ambulances to forget the rules and break the cordon thrown around the area by the police. Severed body parts littered the pavements.

Fleeing the scene in the opposite direction, Babe found a replica of the previous mall, ravaged this time by the Tottenham Boys. At last, his legs still trembling under him, and carrying a few meagre rations overlooked by others, he got clear of the riot zone, his mind still pre-occupied by Madonna-Jo. Would she have seen him on TV? By the time he had fled as far as Brighton he was out of provisions; but he had heard that this was a place of great wealth, and that the inhabitants were progressive, and he was confident that he would fit in there as he had at Sir Digby's, before Madonna-Jo's wonderful eyes had caused his expulsion.

He asked for help from several well-dressed personages on their way home from church who all told him that, if he carried on like this, he would be locked up until he had learnt to stop sponging off others.

Then he joined a large open-air meeting of the homeless and impoverished at which a gentleman spent an hour speaking non-stop on the subject of brotherhood. At the end Babe approached the orator who glanced doubtfully at him and asked, 'What are you doing here? Are you here for the right reasons?'

'The rightness of my reasons is evident,' said Babe modestly, 'from the size of the support which the meeting has engendered: everything which is popular with the majority is of necessity right. It was the will of the people that I should be chased from the arms of Miss Thunder-Smith, that I should be lashed, that I should have to beg a crust until I can earn my living; my association with all these other people demonstrates that it could not but be so.'

'Young man,' said the orator, 'do you believe that Nelson Mandela is an alien sent from the far edges of our galaxy to save us from right-wing tyranny?'

'No-one has ever told me that,' replied Babe, 'but, whichever way it is, I'm hungry.'

'You don't deserve to eat,' was the response. 'Clear off, you wretch, and never let me see you again.'

The orator's wife, happening to overhear the view expressed that Nelson Mandela might be a mere human being, broke a bottle of gin over his head. Oh dear, the ladies lose all sense of proportion when their heroes are maligned!

A man called Max, who was just back from a year's voluntary work in Glasgow, and therefore out of touch with current thinking, saw the cruel and ignominious manner in which his fellow social outcast was being treated, and that man a six-footer in his socks and with a soul to match; he took him back to his flat, cleaned him up, gave him pizza and beer, put some money in his pocket, and even offered to get him employment in the Oxfam shop in Brighton. Babe embraced him, saying, 'Mr Lamode was right when he told me to beware of married couples who espouse causes along with each other. You have shown far greater brotherliness than that other couple, much as I admire their designer clothes.'

The next day, out for a walk, he bumped into a beggar covered in sores, his eyes glazed, his nose red, his mouth twisted, his teeth black, hacking and coughing and croaking, ejecting a tooth with each cough.

4

How Babe met his former teacher, Fabio Lamode,
and what emerged.

Babe, more moved than horrified, gave this awful beggar
the money he had received from the retired businessman,
Max. The apparition stared at him, burst into tears and
flung his arms around his neck. Babe recoiled in horror.

'Oh, I say,' said the one miserable wretch to the other,
'can it be that you do not recognise your dear old Fabio?'

'What's that you say? You, my old teacher, you in this
awful state! Whatever misfortune has befallen you? How
come you are so far from that trendiest of all homes? What
has become of Madonna-Jo, that jewel among girls, that
masterpiece of evolution?' 'I'm too far gone to talk,'
gasped Fabio.

Babe at once took him for shelter to the garages of the
block where Max lived and revived him with a Mars bar.
Once Fabio had recovered he said, 'Ah, my friend, your
Madonna-Jo? She died.'

Babe fainted right away; his friend revived him by
waving under his nose some turps he found on a shelf.
Babe opened his eyes.

'Madonna-Jo, dead! These things do not happen to girls
in Notting Hill. What on earth did she die of? Was it of a
broken heart at seeing me chased from the premises at the
toe-end of her father's Adinikes?'

'No,' said Fabio. 'According to the *Sun* she was

11

disembowelled by some of the Hackney Family after they had exhausted themselves raping her. They broke her father's skull when he tried to defend her; Lady Petal they cut to pieces; the poor little boy suffered exactly the same fate as his sister. As to the house, it was burnt to the ground, there is nothing left. But the *Daily Mirror* reported that Rasta Joe's house had suffered a similar fate at the hands of the Tottenham Boys that same evening.'

Hearing all this, Babe fainted again, but having come round and having said all that he felt moved to say, he enquired as to what in the world had gone wrong to reduce Fabio to this pitifully diminished condition.

'Ah,' was the reply, 'it was sex. Desire, that imperious driver of the human condition, that preserver of the species, that marketing man's dream.'

'Alas,' said Babe, 'I too have known desire, but only in the context of the most pure love; all I had from it was a few kisses and twenty kicks up the backside. How did something so marketable reduce you to such an appalling state?'

Fabio replied after this fashion: 'Oh, my dear Babe! You remember Felicita, our employers' pretty gardener? Between her legs I tasted bliss, a bliss which brought me to the wretched condition in which you see me now; it had infected her … she's probably already dead of it. Felicita contracted it from a well-known designer who had evidently traced its origins, because he knew he'd acquired it from an elderly film-star, who had got it from a journalist, who had been infected by a stand-up comedienne, who got it from a roadie, to whom it had been passed by a student who had done VSO and who could trace its descent in a direct line back to Cecil Rhodes' manservant. But I shall pass it to nobody, because I am dying of it.'

12

'Fabio,' ejaculated Babe, 'what a strange genealogy! Is it not homosexuality that causes the disease?'

'Oh no,' replied that well-informed and worldly gentleman. 'It is a necessary adjunct of our lifestyle. Of course it is true that that this scourge does endanger the procreation of our fashionable people and is the antithesis of what all progressive beings desire, but if Cecil Rhodes hadn't taken his manservant to catch it in the middle of Africa, we would not have had the gold and diamonds with which we are accustomed to adorn our ears and noses. It is true that it is largely unknown amongst some groups of people – accountants for example, school-teachers, solicitors, scientists, plumbers and the like – but no doubt they will catch up with it in the years to come. In the meantime it is making wonderful progress amongst those of our world. When we witness trendy youngsters battling for control of our streets and our buying habits, we can be sure that a third of them will already have succumbed to the syndrome.'

'That's all very well,' said Babe, 'but we must get you some treatment.'

'How do you suggest we do that?' said Fabio. 'I wouldn't be seen dead in a National Health Service hospital. I haven't a penny to my name, and not a single one of the private health schemes I belonged to covers me for this condition.'

The pitifulness of this last admission made up Babe's mind for him. He went and begged for help from that retired businessman Max. Such a sad picture did Babe paint to him of the condition to which his friend was reduced that the good man took Fabio into his flat and procured treatment for him at his own expense. Fabio's condition improved dramatically and he lost only the use of one ear and one eye. He could still use a keyboard and still understand a spreadsheet. The businessman gave him a job as his bookkeeper. A couple of months later, needing to go to San Francisco in connection with some investments, he took the two scholars with him. En route Fabio explained to him the perfection of the American way of life.

Max disagreed. 'It is inevitable,' he said, 'that Americans should find themselves to some extent corrupt and corruptive. They have not evolved in the manner of wolves, but wolves they have become. Nature has not endowed them with super-powerful cars and planes and air-conditioning systems with which to destroy their world, but they have created them. Not to mention the bankers who lend what they haven't got to those who have no possibility of repaying their debt.'

'But that is all indispensable,' replied the one-eyed pedagogue. 'How else are we to rise above the mundane and create the joy of ownership on which we thrive?'

As he was speaking the 'Fasten seat-belts' lights went on, the plane plummeted and rose again, and the lights of San Francisco came into view.

5

Storm, crash-landing, earthquake, and what
became of Fabio Lamode, of Babe, and of Max
the retired businessman amidst it all.

Half of the frightened passengers barely had the presence
of mind to be fully aware of the danger they were in, so
prey were they to that amazing anguish of the soul and of
the stomach which the plummeting of a plane brings. The
other half resorted to praying or to their mobile phones,
switching them back on (illegal and, under the
circumstances, potentially dangerous as it was) to discover
which terrorist group was responsible for the outrage.
Max stood up to try to talk some sense into them, but was
felled by a blow from the riot-stick of an undercover
security guard. The plane landed on the Interstate with a
force which smashed the undercarriage and left it skidding
on its belly in a shower of sparks. Struggling to his feet,
Max saw the security guard's clothes catching fire.
Leaping to his assistance he was able to half smother the
flames and push him out through a hole in the fuselage on
to the road. Max was too late to follow and was engulfed
in the inferno. Besides the security guard, the only other
ones to make it out on to the road were Babe and Fabio,
who, by rolling down an embankment into a field, put out
the smouldering parts of their garments.

   Barely knowing what they were doing, Babe and Fabio,
accompanied by the security guard, walked in the

direction of the city. Having escaped the plane crash, they hoped they had enough money on them to buy some kind of food and shelter, however utilitarian.

Still upset by the death of their benefactor, they stumbled into the city of San Francisco, to the amazement of the locals who rarely saw even down-and-outs (as these clearly were) on foot and not in cars. Suddenly they seemed to be reliving the nightmare of the moments before the plane crash, as the ground began to rise and fall beneath them. Buildings collapsed, roads split, fires broke out, cars ran out of control: 300,000 people died. The security guard darted off, tear-gas gun at the ready, saying he would soon get the heathen bastards who had done this. He was distracted, though, by the possibilities of stores opened defenceless to any passer-by, and was soon drunkenly comforting a rather attractive teenager who had asked him to look for her pussy. Fabio tapped him on the shoulder and suggested that his duty was to preserve the safety and security of the public.

'Hell's bells!' was the reply. 'It was the airline was paying me, not the public. Screw the public.' And he was as good as his word.

Babe had been injured by some falling masonry and lay in the street covered in rubble. He called to Fabio, 'Get me some wine and some morphine, I'm dying.'

'I recall hearing of other earthquakes,' said Fabio. 'There was one in China last year. It must be the effect of global warming. There must be a hole in the ozone layer above the Pacific.'

'Very possibly,' said Babe, 'but please can I have some wine and morphine?'

'What do you mean 'possibly'?' said the pedagogue. 'It's obvious. I don't need an opinion poll to demonstrate the truth of what I'm saying.'

Babe lost consciousness, and Fabio procured him a sip of water from a puddle.

The next day they found some shops still not emptied where they could source something to restore their strength. Then they joined in the rescue effort. Some of the people they helped dig out of their ruined homes rewarded them by sharing what food they could salvage. They were miserable at the poverty of what they could offer and at the lack of air-conditioning. Fabio comforted them with the assurance that if global warming had caused an earthquake in San Francisco the effect was being felt there and not in Washington, so it could have been worse.

A large, red-necked man with a sticker on his sleeve proclaiming 'Coffee-Party' said politely, 'It would appear that the gentleman does not believe that this destruction is a good and necessary part of God's Intelligent Design.'

'Indeed, I crave your indulgence,' said Fabio even more politely, 'but it is clear that it is by chance that Americans have evolved to create global warming and thus earthquakes.'

'So you do not believe in the rightness of the American Dream?'

'I'm sorry,' replied Fabio, 'but the dream of perfection co-exists with the evolution of the seeds of its own destruction, in that...'

But before he could finish his sentence the American had turned away to ask if no-one had any goddam whiskey.

6

How a really effective interrogation was contrived with a view to preventing any more earthquakes, and how Babe came to lose his skin again.

As a result of the earthquake which had destroyed a large part of San Francisco, the authorities set about reassuring the remnants of the population that they were taking all possible measures to prevent a re-occurrence: they would show on live television the results of their enquiries.

They already had in custody an immigrant from Saudi Arabia accused of entering into a forced marriage, and they seized two men of Arab appearance who were reported hunting for halal meat; then they took Fabio and his pupil Babe, the one for saying too much and the other for listening with every sign of approval. They were all rendered on a boat to the island of Alcatraz, which had been closed to the general public for the occasion. There they were incarcerated in solitary confinement in damp, dingy, airless cells for a week under the constant gaze of the TV cameras. The populace enjoyed noisy demonstrations of hatred for them in the ruined streets. When they were considered suitably impressed, they were dressed in Arab garments and given copies of the Koran to hold whilst they were herded through a line of five hundred press and TV cameramen gathered together from around the western world. Their walk ended at an installation specially designed to enable a smooth transition from the waterboarding ceremony to the electric chair. A one-thousand-strong choir of cheerleaders representing every baseball and football team in the USA danced and sang to one side whilst the waterboarding was carried out. The three 'Arabs' of course confessed and were electrocuted. Fabio was drowned, which the President insisted was an unusual and unavoidable accident. Then it was Babe's turn and, having remarkable lungs, he was able to exasperate his interrogators. They fired the electric current, but when Babe merely sustained extensive burns the crowd pronounced him innocent and let him go. The same evening the city suffered an enormous aftershock.

Babe, horrified, dazed, skinless, breathless, wondered: 'If this is the most progressive of countries, what must the others be like? OK, I've lost my skin, but that happened to me before in London; but dear Fabio, best of teachers, did I have to see you drowned without understanding what law of fashionable opinion you had transgressed? Dear businessman, best of men, what had you done to deserve being burnt to death? Madonna-Jo, jewel amongst girls, why did the will of the people cause you to be disembowelled like that?'

He was wandering in his mind as well as with his feet, barely able to stand, with fifty per cent burns, not knowing what to believe, in a most unfashionable and simple state, when he was accosted by an elderly-looking lady who said, 'Young man, do not despair. Follow me.'

7

How an elderly lady looked after Babe, and how he rediscovered that which he loved.

Babe was not greatly encouraged, but followed the old dear nevertheless to a room in a tenement block. She gave him lard to rub on himself and something to eat and drink. Then she showed him to a reasonably clean bed, beside which lay a full set of workaday clothes.

'Eat, drink, sleep,' she said to him, 'and may your dreams be of caviar, Pimms and Armani. I'll be back tomorrow.'

Babe, still struggling to comprehend all he had seen and suffered, and still more amazed at the kindness of the elderly woman, tried to kiss her cheek.

'It's not me you need to kiss,' said the lady. 'I'll see you again tomorrow. Rub some grease on your burns, eat and sleep.'

Babe, in spite of his pain, did eat and sleep. The next day the woman brought him breakfast, tended to his wounds, herself applying a proper salve to the burns. Later she brought him some dinner, and in the evening some supper. The next day the same.

'Who are you?' Babe kept asking her. 'Why are you being so good to me? How can I repay you?'

The good woman would make no reply. But when she returned the next evening she was not bearing any supper. 'Come with me,' she said, 'but keep quiet.'

She took his arm and led him to a leafy suburb. They approached a house set in a large garden with manicured lawns and many water features. The old lady knocked at a side door: it was opened and she preceded Babe up a narrow spiral staircase into a room decorated in the Scandinavian style, left him sitting on a luxurious sofa, and disappeared, closing the door after her. Babe thought he must be dreaming, that all his life had been one long and dismal nightmare transformed at present into a happy dream.

But then, picture this: the elderly lady reappears. She is giving her arm to a trembling, stumbling female figure, wonderfully attired, sparkling with real jewels, her face veiled.

'You may remove the veil,' says the old lady to Babe.

The young man approaches; shyly he lifts the veil. What a sensation! What a moment to treasure! He seems to be seeing the face of Madonna-Jo! His strength fails him, he cannot speak, he falls to his knees. Madonna-Jo collapses on to the sofa. The old lady supplies reviving spirits; they come to their senses. They talk, at first disjointedly, their questions and answers intermingling; there are sighs, there are tears, there are shrieks. The old lady advises them to keep the noise down and leaves them to themselves.

'It really is you,' exclaimed Babe. 'You're alive! To think I should find you again here, of all places, in San Francisco! So the media got it wrong? You weren't raped? They didn't disembowel you, as our teacher Fabio believed?'

'Oh it did happen,' said the beautiful Madonna-Jo, 'but sometimes one can survive such treatment.'

'And your father and mother, were they killed?'

'That is only too true,' said Madonna-Jo, weeping again.

'And your brother?'

'My brother died too.'

'So how do you come to be in California? And how did you learn of my presence here? And what mysterious chance allowed you to have me brought here?'

'I will explain it all,' replied the girl, 'but first you must tell me everything that has happened to you since those innocent kisses you gave me and those kicks you received.'

Babe was obedient to her wishes, and, stupefied as he was, weak and trembling as was his voice, sore and painful as was his body, he contrived to recount in the simplest of terms all he had undergone since they had been parted. Madonna-Jo repeatedly closed her eyes in sympathy; she shed tears at the deaths of the retired businessman and of Fabio. Then she spoke to Babe as follows, and Babe listened, transfixed by her words and by her beauty.

8

Madonna-Jo's story.

'I was fast asleep in my bed when the envy in the hearts of the Hackney Family led them to invade our beautiful 'Sunday-supplement' home. They stabbed my father and brother, killing them, and cut my mother to shreds. A seven-foot tall gang member, seeing that I had fainted at the horror of it, set about raping me; this brought me back to my senses. I screamed, I fought, I bit, I scratched, I tried to claw out the youth's eyes: I had no conception that what was happening in my father's house was a normal occurrence in an affordable home. The yob stuck a knife in my side, I still bear the scar.'

'Oh, I hope I shall get to see it!' said Babe with utter simplicity.

'You shall,' said Madonna-Jo, 'but for the moment let me continue my story.'

'Do,' said Babe.

She resumed thus: 'One of the gang leaders saw what was happening; he berated the gang member for not showing more respect, and knifed him through the heart. Then he had my wounds dressed by one of his "sisters" and took me back to his pad. I had to prepare his meals and do his cleaning. He found me very attractive, I have to tell you, and I don't deny that I found him very well-built and with a well-muscled body. What was more, he didn't think or talk much: he clearly had not had the benefit of a

23

tutor such as Mr Lamode. After I'd been there three months he grew tired of me and of having to pay for my upkeep, and passed me on to a Russian oligarch called Magnatovich, who dealt between America and Europe. He loved girls generally and really had the hots for me, but he didn't get anywhere. I put up more resistance to him than I had to the gangster. A well brought-up girl may be taken advantage of once, but she learns to protect herself. Seeking to impress me, the oligarch had me flown to the mansion where you find me. I had thought that my father's house was the finest in the world: I have learnt differently.

'A media tycoon saw me one day in a nightclub the oligarch liked to take me to. He kept looking at me, then gave me to understand he wanted to interview me himself, personally. I was taken to his office. I told him something of my origins. He suggested to me that being the mistress of a Russian oligarch was not the best I could do for myself. He put pressure on Magnatovich, seeking a transfer deal. Magnatovich, considering himself to be media-proof, declared he wasn't interested. The media tycoon threatened to make him look lower than the meanest politician. In the end my Russian made a deal whereby this mansion and I would be shared equally between them: the Russian would have access to me on Mondays, Wednesdays and Saturdays, and the media tycoon would get the other days of the week. This has been the position for the last few months. There have been occasional disputes: it's not always clear whether the night of Saturday to Sunday belongs to the one or to the other. As for my own person, so far I have always refused to go all the way with either man, and I think that is why they are so infatuated with me.

'Then, in order to ward off more earthquakes, and also to intimidate Magnatovich, the media tycoon caused the

24

public trial to be laid on. He did me the honour of inviting me. I had an excellent view. Between the trial and the executions they served the guests a superb buffet. It has to be said that I was pretty horrified at witnessing the deaths of the two Arabs, and of the Saudi who had entered into a forced marriage; but imagine my surprise, my anguish, my horror when I saw, dressed in Arab robes and with a towel on his head, a man who looked like Mr Lamode! I rubbed my eyes and peered at him again. I saw him drowned. I went weak at the knees. Hardly had I recovered myself than there you were, naked as the day you were born. I was in the height of mental agony, of sorrow, of despair. I have to say to you, in all honesty, that your musculature compares well with that of the gang-leader. This realisation served only to redouble the emotions which consumed me. I cried out, I wanted to scream that they should stop but I could not find my voice and it would have been pointless anyway. When I saw you being electrocuted …! How can it be, I said to myself, that dear Babe and clever Fabio should turn up in San Francisco, the one to be electrocuted, the other to be drowned, and this at the whim of a media tycoon who adores me? Fabio Lamode cruelly misled me when he taught me that the world had evolved over time towards perfection.

'I was close to a nervous breakdown, beside myself, one moment in hysterics, the next almost fainting. My head was full of the massacre of my father and mother and brother, of the insolence of that vicious gangster and of the cut he gave me, of my time keeping house and cooking for my gang-leader, of my wicked Magnatovich, of my abominable media tycoon, of the drowning of Fabio Lamode, of the chants of the cheerleaders while you were being interrogated, but most of all of the kiss you gave me behind the screen the day I saw you last. It seemed a miracle that I should find you again after all those horrible experiences. I asked my companion to look after you and to bring you here as soon as she could. She did brilliantly. I have had the incredible pleasure of seeing you again, of hearing your voice and of being able to talk to you. You must be starving; I'm certainly hungry. Let's have something to eat.'

So the two of them sat at the table, and when they had dined they went back to recline on the magnificent sofa mentioned earlier. And that is where they were when Mr Magnatovich, one of the owners of the mansion, came in. It was a Saturday. He had come to enjoy that to which he considered himself entitled, and to give expression to his devotion.

9

*What became of Madonna-Jo, of Babe, of the
oligarch, and of the tycoon.*

This Magnatovich had the worst temper of any Russian
since Stalin. 'What's this?' he cried. 'You perfidious bitch,
is the tycoon not enough for you? You want me to share
you with this rascal too?'

So saying he pulled out the knife he always carried and,
assuming his adversary to be unarmed, flung himself on
Babe. But our good Brit. had been provided as a matter of
course with a gun amongst the American clothes put out
for him. Gentle as his manners normally were, he drew out
the gun and in a trice the oligarch was lying dead on the
floor at Madonna-Jo's feet.

'Heavens above!' she screamed. 'What will become of us?
A man is killed in my room. If the law turns up, we've had it.'

'If only Fabio hadn't been drowned,' said Babe, 'he
would have had good advice for us in this extremity; he
always taught us the right thing to do. Since he isn't here,
let us ask your companion what she thinks.'

She was a very prudent lady, and was just about to
deliver her opinion when a door to one side opened. It was
1.00 a.m., the early hours of Sunday morning. This was
one of the tycoon's days. In he came, and saw Babe, whose
interrogation he had witnessed, with a gun in his hand, a
man lying dead on the floor, Madonna-Jo looking
terrified, and the old lady giving advice.

27

This is what went through Babe's heart and mind at this juncture: 'If this public figure calls the police, it is inevitable that I shall end up in the electric chair, and quite possibly Madonna-Jo will too; he's already caused me to be brutally interrogated; he is my rival in love; I've just killed one person: it's a no-brainer.' His mind reasoned all this in a split second, and before the tycoon could recover from his surprise he was lying dead next to the oligarch, shot through the heart.

'So, there's another nail in our coffin,' said Madonna-Jo. 'That's done for us. We can't plead extenuating circumstances now. Our goose is cooked! Whatever possessed you, born as you were to be a gentleman, to kill within the space of two minutes a rich Russian and a rich American?'

'My dear,' replied Babe, 'when a man is in love, jealous, and recovering from an interrogation, that man does not behave normally.'

Then the companion spoke up. 'There's a Porsche in the garage, with a full tank of gas: Babe must go and get it out. The young lady has jewellery and her credit card. Let's all get in the car, even if I can sit comfortably only on one buttock, and let's head down the coast. It's a lovely moonlit night for a drive. The view out over the Pacific will be wonderful.'

Babe got the car out and off they went. Whilst they were driving the Red Cross entered the house: in due course the tycoon was cremated with great ceremony, the oligarch thrown into a mass grave with other earthquake victims.

By then Babe, Madonna-Jo and her companion had already arrived in Santa Ana, and over breakfast in a diner were having the following conversation ...

10

*The state of distress in which Babe, Madonna-Jo
and the old lady arrive in San Diego, and their
setting sail.*

'Who could have stolen my credit card and jewellery?'
wailed Madonna-Jo. 'What shall we live on? How shall we
manage? Where shall I find oligarchs and tycoons to
replenish my resources?'

'I'm afraid,' said the companion, 'that I suspect those
two girls in the motel in Gover City who were on their
way to the film studios to start work on a film with Brad
Holl. They came into our room a couple of times to show
us photos of themselves with various film-stars. And they
checked out very early, before breakfast.'

'Oh dear!' said Babe. 'Our dear friend Fabio told us that
it became the rich to give to charity, and not to expect too
much publicity for it. Those girls had only to ask for
sponsorship, they didn't need to steal all we had. Do you
really have nothing left, my sweetheart?'

'Not a cent,' was the reply.

'What's our best course of action?' asked Babe.

'I propose we part-exchange the Porsche for a couple of
motorcycles,' said the companion. 'It will be less
comfortable for me, since I have only one buttock to sit
on, but we'll have what we need to get to San Diego.'

It so happened that a leather-clad biker couple were
staying at the same motel. They consented to part-exchange

their elderly bikes for the Porsche. With Madonna-Jo riding pillion behind the lady on her one buttock the three contrived to make it through to San Diego. There they found that an expeditionary force of volunteers was being assembled under the auspices of Amnesty International, with the assistance of the CIA and funded by Coca Cola, to take on the might of the Columbian drug barons who were accused of making charitable work in their area impossible. Babe, with his training in the Hackney Family behind him, applied to join up. Such was the grace, the skill, the swiftness, and the agility with which he completed the tasks set to test him, that he was not only enlisted but given the rank of captain. When he boarded the ship he was accompanied by Madonna-Jo, her companion and the two motorbikes he had acquired.

During the voyage they spent much time discussing what poor Fabio had taught them.

'We shall be arriving in a totally different world,' said Babe. 'Perhaps this is where we shall see the full perfection of human evolution. It is, after all, very close to where Darwin started evolution, and perhaps the closer to the source one gets, the better the results.'

'I love and honour you with all my heart,' said Madonna-Jo, 'but I'm still totally unsettled by all that I've seen and had happen to me.'

'We'll be OK,' replied Babe. 'You notice how much more consistent and calm the weather is in the warmth of this part of the globe than it was all the way over there in Europe. It must be that here everything has evolved to perfection.'

'I do hope so,' said Madonna-Jo, 'but I've been so horribly unhappy elsewhere that I can feel but little hope in my heart.'

'You think you are hard done by,' said her companion. 'Your sufferings are as nothing compared with mine.'

Madonna-Jo had the greatest difficulty in stopping herself laughing out loud at the idea that this sweet old lady could have known greater suffering than her. 'My dear,' she told her, 'unless you've been raped by *two* gangsters, unless you've seen *two* homes demolished around you, unless you've witnessed *two* sets of parents having their throats cut, unless you've seen *two* lovers placed under interrogation, I don't understand how you can claim to be the greater sufferer; add to that the fact that I, who was born to Platinum Credit Cards, found myself doing ironing for someone else.'

'Young lady,' replied the older one, 'you know nothing of my origins; and if I were to show you my backside, you would lose your prejudice.'

Her words aroused great curiosity in Babe and Madonna-Jo, and this the older lady set about satisfying, as follows.

11

The companion's story.

'I didn't always have these red-rimmed, wrinkled eyes; there was a time when my nose didn't touch my chin; I wasn't always a charlady. I am the daughter of the international footballer Gavin Rookham and of the pop-singer Cherie Yellowhammer. Until I was fourteen I lived in a mansion so big your father's house would have fitted into the garage, and one of my dresses cost more than that Porsche. I was raised to be beautiful, graceful, talented, happy, respected, ambitious. Boys fell at my feet. My breasts formed – white, firm, shaped like those of the Venus de Milo. And my eyes! My eyelashes! My eyebrows were jet black; my eyes sparkled from under them, outshining the stars as my mother's songwriters put it. My masseuse and manicurist would swoon in ecstasy as I undressed, whether they were viewing me from in front or behind, and there wasn't a man who did not wish he could change places with them.

'I became engaged to the son of a Sheikh. He was a prince! As handsome as I was beautiful, steeped in charm and good manners, witty, and ardent in his love. I idolised him, longed for him, as we girls do for our first love. The wedding arrangements were made. Such a magnificent occasion had never been seen: fountains of champagne, the guests to be flown in by helicopter and private jet, dancing in the evening for which The Rolling Stones were to re-form to do songs written specially in my honour, the whole thing to be broadcast live on every subscription channel in the world. I could not have been happier. But then a cast-off lover of my fiancé who had the misfortune to be a couple of years older than me invited him to have one last glass of Bolly with her. It took him two hours of agony to die. But that's a minor detail. My mother, in despair (though not quite to the degree I was) decided we needed to get away from the scene of the disaster. She took me on our yacht to cruise the Indian Ocean. Suddenly, a launch containing pirates roared up and they boarded us. Our bodyguards performed heroically, promising to waive any claims for compensation if they were released at once.

'In a trice all we ladies, including my mother, were stripped as naked as the apes from which we've evolved. It had to be seen to be believed, the diligence with which those gentlemen went about their task of stripping the clothes off us. But what was even more surprising to me was that they set about inserting their fingers into places where we ladies normally put only objects designed for the purpose. I judged this a very odd ceremony, but I suppose one is automatically prejudiced to assume the customs of one's own country. I subsequently discovered that it was in order to ensure we had no diamonds hidden away there, and that it had been normal practice since time immemorial amongst the seafaring peoples of the world; I was told that the crew of no UN patrol boat would fail to do likewise when boarding the vessels of potential smugglers: it is a basic human right and duty which is not to be ignored.

'I'm sure I don't have to spell out to you how hard it is for a young rich girl to find herself enslaved in North Africa along with her mother. You can imagine the treatment meted out to us on the pirate vessel. My mother was still very beautiful. The other ladies of the volunteer force were perceived as having more beauty between them than all the native ladies of North Africa put together. As for me, I enchanted them as the epitome of grace and beauty – and I was still a virgin. I didn't remain one for long! That flower, reserved for the handsome Prince Abu-Massa-Carrera, was plucked by the pirate captain, a conceited brute who boasted that I should be honoured to be deflowered by him. It took enormous strength of character on the part of my mother and myself to cope with all we had to endure before reaching port; but there we are, these hardships are so common-or-garden they hardly warrant a mention.

'When we arrived we found Somalia positively swimming in blood. Every one of fifty separate Islamic factions, each with its own militia, was claiming to have the right to form the government. This meant in effect fifty simultaneous civil wars: sect against sect, tribe against tribe, family against family. Throughout the land it was one continual slaughter.

'Hardly had we disembarked than members of a faction opposed to my pirate captain turned up to seize his plunder. After the food and computers and money, we ladies were the most valuable items of his booty. I witnessed a battle such as you would never see in modern European civilisation. Northerners simply do not possess the same fire in their blood; they do not hunger after women in the way that Equatorial peoples do. The blood of your European runs with milk: it is fire and brimstone which courses through the veins of the peoples of the Sahara and the neighbouring areas. They fought over us in the fashion of the savage fauna of the region. One tribesman seized my mother by the right arm, my captain's Mate got her by the left; one landsman seized her by the one leg, one of the pirates held her by the other. Before you could blink all the women found themselves similarly in the hands of four combatants. My captain kept me hidden behind him. With his fist he could populate a cemetery; it was death to come within range of his rage. Finally, every one of our group, including my mother, lay torn and cut to pieces, massacred by these quarrelling monsters. The captives and those who captured them – every single one, including my captain – all were dead, and I was left at death's door myself, lying amidst a pile of corpses. It is a well-known fact that similar scenes have occurred across the lands from Algeria to Iraq without a single one of the five prayers a day ordered by the Prophet being missed.

'With great difficulty I struggled free of the bloody heap of bodies and dragged myself into the shade of a large orange tree growing next to a stream. There I collapsed, overwhelmed by horror, by weariness of spirit, by despair and by hunger. Soon I succumbed to a sleep which had more about it of unconsciousness than of rest. It was while I was in this state of senseless weakness, neither properly living nor properly dead, that I became aware of something pressing down and agitating itself on my body. I opened my eyes and saw the face of a good-looking white man sighing and murmuring, "Jesus, it's so tough to be impotent!"'

12

Continuation of the companion's story.

'Amazed and delighted to hear my native tongue being spoken, I replied that there were greater misfortunes than that to which he alluded. I was able to give him a brief account of the afflictions I had suffered, before lapsing back into semi-consciousness. He carried me to a nearby house, put me to bed, looked after me, consoled me, flattered me, told me I was the most beautiful creature he had ever seen and that he had never regretted so much being without that which no-one could give back to him.

'"I was born in New York," he told me. "There they use drugs on two to three thousand children a year in an effort to ensure that they will grow into outstanding athletes: some do, some die, some, like me, suffer crippling side-effects. Some do thrive as athletes, win Olympic medals and go on to become diplomats, film-stars, or even State Governors. Apart from my little problem I thrived, and was accepted into the training camp run by the great Gavin Rookham, where I became a favourite of the wonderful Cherie Yellowhammer."

'"Of my mother!" I exclaimed.

'"Your mother!" he ejaculated with tears in his eyes. "Can this be true? Are you the little Tiffany I played with so regularly till you were six years old, and who had already shown the promise of turning into the beauty you are?"

'"I am she. My mother is to be found just a few hundred yards from here lying under a pile of bodies, torn into four pieces."

'I told him all that had happened to me. He in turn related his adventures: how upon his retirement from sport he had been sent by the CIA as an emissary to Somalia to seek an arms deal whereby Somalia would receive planes, tanks and guns to turn eventually on America's allies, who are also their business rivals, and disrupt their trade.

'"I have completed my mission," said this honest eunuch. "Now I must leave for home, and I shall take you with me. Oh, it's so tough being impotent!"

'I thanked him with tears for his kindness. Instead of taking me home, he took me to the Sudan and sold me to an elderly sheikh. The purchase was barely concluded when the tuberculosis epidemic broke out that decimated so much of Africa, Asia and Europe. If only science had not taught us to overuse antibiotics! You have experienced earthquakes; but, young lady, I bet you have never known tuberculosis?'

'No, I haven't,' replied Madonna-Jo.

'If you had,' pursued the companion whose name was Tiffany, 'you would have to admit that it's worse than an earthquake. It's inescapable in Africa. It attacked me. Put yourself in the position of a well-brought-up young heiress who, within the space of three months, has experienced poverty, slavery, daily rape, her mother torn in four before her eyes, has known hunger and warfare, and who now finds herself in Khartoum dying of tuberculosis. But I didn't die. My vendor and my purchaser and the whole of the sheikh's entourage perished, though.

'Once the worst was over the slaves were sold off. I was bought by a trader who took me to Algiers. He sold me to another merchant who found a buyer for me in Tripoli.

From there I was passed to someone in Alexandria, was handed on to a man in Damascus and from Damascus was transported to Kabul. I ended up in the entourage of a Taleban warlord who was soon sent to fight the Russians.

'The warlord, who was a great one for the ladies, took all his girls with him and kept us in a mosque under the guard of twenty soldiers. Huge numbers of Russians were killed, but they gave as good as they got. Herat was reduced to rubble; by chance, the building we were being kept in was the only one left standing. Rather than risk needless lives attacking a mosque, the Russians decided to leave a small detachment to starve us out. The twenty Taleban soldiers had sworn never to surrender. Rather than break their oath they decided they would have to eat us.

'There was an Imam with us, a most holy and compassionate man. He preached a fine sermon which persuaded them not to kill us outright.

'"All you need to do," he said, "is cut one buttock from each of these girls: cook that and it will be more than adequate to keep you going. If necessary, in a few days the other side will still be available. But Heaven will reward you for your charity and rescue will come."

'A most eloquent man, he won them over. They performed this ghastly operation on each of us. The Imam treated our wounds with the same ointment as is used on babies when they have been circumcised. We were all at death's door.

'As it turned out scarcely had the Taleban eaten their meal than the Russians burst in. Not one member of the Taleban was spared. The Russians paid no attention to the state we were in. But *Médecin sans Frontières* crops up everywhere. A British medic working with them treated our wounds most skilfully and soon had us fit again. I shall never forget as long as I live how, once my wounds were healed, he made me certain overtures. Apart from that he tried hard to console us all, telling us that such things were by no means uncommon and must be considered a normal consequence of involvement in warfare.

'Once we could all walk we were taken off to Moscow. I was allocated to a Party official who had me tend his garden and gave me twenty strokes of the cane every day, just for fun. But this gentleman was accused some two years later of obscure offences against the Party and he disappeared. I took advantage of the confusion to run away. I succeeded in crossing Russia and getting over the border into the EU. For some time I worked as a barmaid in a nightclub in Riga. Then I made my way via Copenhagen, Hamburg, Leipzig, Hannover, Utrecht, Leyden and The Hague to Amsterdam. I was aged by the misery of my hand-to-mouth existence and the disdain shown me. Awareness of my plight – me, the daughter of wealth reduced to having only one buttock – made me long for death. Yet here I am, alive. This survival instinct is a dreadful hardship upon us all. What could be worse than this compulsion to go on bearing a burden which one longs to hurl to the ground? What worse fate than to abominate one's own existence, whilst yet clinging to it? Being forced to stroke the beast that is devouring us until it has consumed its last morsel?

'During the course of my wanderings and in the bars where I served, I came across any number of people who held their very existence to be an abomination, but I met only twelve who chose to put an end to their torment: three Africans, four Englishman, four Swiss, and one German professor. I ended up in the household of the media tycoon who bade me look after you, young lady. I grew very fond of you and have been more preoccupied with your troubles than with my own. I still would not have mentioned my misfortunes to you, had it not been for your winding me up a bit and for the custom on cruise ships of sharing life stories with one's fellow passengers to keep boredom at bay. So, I have some experience of life and of the world. I challenge you: ask each person on board to tell you their history and I bet you will not find one who has not cursed his or her very existence, who does not see him or herself as the most unfortunate person in the world. If I'm wrong, chuck me overboard!'

13

How Babe was obliged to allow himself to be separated from Madonna-Jo and the old lady.

Having listened to the old lady's story, the beautiful Madonna-Jo paid her all the compliments which are due to a person of such rank and merit in society. She took up the challenge: one after the other she persuaded all the other passengers to tell their life stories. Babe and she had to admit that the old lady was right.

'It is a real shame,' observed Babe, 'that wise Fabio was drowned contrary to normal usage in the course of his interrogation. He would have had such interesting things to say on the origins of the physical and moral ills of the current world population, and I would feel myself to be in a position to question respectfully some of his assumptions.'

Whilst all these stories were being told, the ship was making progress and they disembarked in Buenaventura. Madonna-Jo, Babe and the companion found themselves in the presence of the Chief of Police, Don Fernando d'Ibarao y Figuera y Mascarenso y Lampourdos y Souza. This gentleman was possessed of the overweening pride to be expected of the bearer of so many names. He spoke with such haughty disdain whilst looking down his nose at his interlocutor, speaking pitilessly loudly and in such a domineering tone, adopting the while such an overbearing pose, that everyone who fell into conversation with him ended up being tempted to hit him. He had a passion for the female sex and Madonna-Jo struck him as the most beautiful woman he had ever seen. Straight off, he asked if she wasn't perhaps Captain Babe's wife. The manner of his putting the question thoroughly alarmed Babe. He didn't quite dare to claim her as his wife, because she wasn't. He didn't dare say she was his sister, because she wasn't exactly that either, and whilst there have been, and are, social situations where such a subterfuge may be considered a useful and acceptable ploy, Babe's soul was too pure to admit of such a lie.

'Miss Thunder-Smith,' he said, 'is engaged to become my wife, and we should be most grateful if you, Sir, would supply the necessary documents, then do us the honour of acting as my best man.'

Don Fernando d'Ibarao y Figuera y Mascarenso y Lampourdos y Souza twirled his moustache, smiled unpleasantly, and told Captain Babe he should go and review his troops. Babe did as he was commanded; the Chief of Police remained with Madonna-Jo. He declared to her his passion and swore he would marry her the next day, in church or out of it, such were her attractions. Madonna-Jo begged a quarter of an hour to reflect, to consult her lady companion, and to make up her mind.

Tiffany said, 'Madonna-Jo, you are possessed of great beauty and of not a cent. You have the opportunity to become the wife of the most powerful man on the continent, a man who sports a very fine moustache. Does it make sense for you to remain faithful, whatever the temptation? You have been raped by gangsters; an oligarch and a tycoon have enjoyed your favours: such misfortunes endow you with certain rights. I have to say, were I in your shoes, I should marry the Chief of Police and so guarantee Babe's wellbeing.'

It was while the lady was speaking thus with all the

42

good sense that comes with age and experience that a helicopter bearing the markings of the American Navy became visible preparing to land – and here is why.

The old lady had correctly deduced that it was the two aspiring actresses who had robbed Madonna-Jo in Gover City in the course of her escape with Babe. The girls tried to use the credit card upon their arrival in Los Angeles. The card was recognised as belonging to the murdered media tycoon. The girls attempted to plea-bargain by naming the persons from whom they had stolen the card and revealing what they knew of their travel plans. Madonna-Jo and Babe were already on the FBI's radar. They were traced as far as San Diego. A signal was sent to a naval patrol vessel to receive on board an FBI lieutenant and to proceed to within helicopter range of Buenaventura. There the word soon spread that the arrest of the murderers of the media tycoon was imminent.

The clever old lady realised at once what had to be done. 'You cannot escape, Madonna-Jo, but you need have nothing to fear; you didn't kill him and anyway the Chief of Police, who is so infatuated with you, will protect you. You stay where you are.'

She hurried off to find Babe.

'Make good your escape,' she said, 'or you're for the electric chair.'

He had not a moment to lose, but how could he bring himself to part from Madonna-Jo and where could he flee to?

14

How Babe and Wayne were received by the
Columbian guerilla forces.

In San Diego Babe had made friends with another
volunteer, a young man of the kind often found amongst
such well-meaning volunteer groups. Of mixed race, born
in a suburb of Cardiff, he had been a Boy Scout, an active
member of Greenpeace and of Amnesty International; he
had completed eighteen months of a degree course in
Sociology at the University of Portsmouth, then had served
in the Army for two years before deserting and making his
way to America. His name was Wayne and he had
recognised in Babe a kindred spirit and a hero. He took it
upon himself swiftly to pack their gear on to the two
motorbikes.

'Come on, mate, let's take the old girl's advice. Let's
clear out and not look back.'

Babe's eyes filled with tears. 'Oh, my darling Madonna-
Jo! Must I really abandon you now, just when our
marriage seems a genuine possibility? Madonna-Jo, so far
from home, what will become of you?'

'She'll manage,' said Wayne. 'Girls always find a way.
Come on!'

'But where can we go? Where do you suggest? How
shall we manage without Madonna-Jo?' was Babe's
constant litany.

'By heck,' said Wayne, 'we were going to make war on

44

the drugs cartels: we'll fight *for* them instead. I've put in a bit of time out here, I think I know how to find their HQ. They'll be thrilled to welcome a captain with your gangland skills. They'll pay you a fortune. You don't make it in one way, you make it in another. That's good – it's educational to try new things in life.'

'So you've been here before?' asked Babe.

'I might've been,' Wayne replied cautiously. 'I was a kind of missionary for a few months and I know the set-up here like the back of my hand. It's brilliant how these guerillas run the show. Their domain covers several hundred square miles and they've divided it into thirty regions. The *Farc* have it all, the ordinary people nothing. It's brilliant. They're so clever, these guerillas. Here they side with the cartels in the war against the Americans, and when they're in the States they live like kings in luxury penthouses. They've got it down to a fine art. Come on! We'll end up living like kings ourselves. They won't be able to do enough for you once they know you're a captain with gangland skills.'

They came to the first of the road-blocks and Babe told the sentry that a captain wished to speak with the Commandant. The guard was turned out and a lieutenant phoned the Commandant. Babe and Wayne were body-searched and their weapons and bikes were seized. They were surrounded by a circle of guards, and the Commandant came and stood outside the circle. He shouted to them that Americans were not welcome there.

'Can't we speak to the Regional Governor?' said Babe.

'The internet connection is only up for an hour a day,' was the reply. 'It will be three o'clock before we can raise him.'

'But,' said Wayne, 'we're both starving hungry and we're not American anyway. Can't we have something to eat while we're waiting?'

45

What Wayne had said was relayed to the Commandant outside the circle.

'Great!' shouted the Commandant. 'Since he's not American I'm allowed to speak to him. Have him brought to my garden room.'

Babe and Wayne were conducted to a beautiful, tree-shaded, marble pergola, amongst the leaves of which twittered all kinds of exotic and colourful birds – budgerigars, parakeets, hummingbirds, guinea-fowl ... goodness knows what else. An excellent meal had been prepared, served on exquisite china. The native people were eating maize from wooden bowls out in the field in the full heat of the sun: meanwhile the Commandant made his entrance into the shady bower.

He was a most handsome young man, his face pale and chubby but with high colour in the cheeks, his eyebrows lofty, his eyes sharp, his ears red, his lips purple – proud of mien but without that Latin swagger. Their weapons were returned to Babe and Wayne, and their motorbikes parked by the door. Wayne negotiated for their tanks to be filled, having in mind that they would be ready should a quick departure be called for.

Babe bowed in the approved fashion to the Commandant and they sat down to table. 'So, you are English?' asked the Commandant.

'Indeed I am, Sir,' said Babe.

As they were speaking, each eyed the other with surprise and growing excitement.

'What part of England are you from?' asked the officer.

'From the accursed neighbourhood of Notting Hill in London,' said Babe. 'I was raised in the famous house of Sir Digby Thunder-Smith.'

'Good Lord! I don't believe this,' exclaimed the Commandant.

'This is incredible!' exclaimed Babe.

'Can it be you?' said the Commandant.

'I don't believe it!' said Babe. Both sprang to their feet, knocking over their chairs, embraced and shed copious tears.

'It's really you, Sir, the brother of my lovely Madonna-Jo! But you were killed by the Hackney Family! You and your parents! And now I discover you leading a group of guerillas in Columbia. This really is a strange world we live in. Oh Fabio, Fabio! If only you hadn't been drowned you would be so happy at this moment.'

The Commandant dismissed the attendants who had been serving fine wine in fine glasses. He and Babe kept falling into each other's arms, their faces wet with tears of joy.

'You will be even more amazed, even more emotional, even more beside yourself with joy when I tell you that your sister Madonna-Jo, whom you believed stabbed to death, is alive and in excellent health.'

'Where?'

'Not far from here, in the house of the Chief of Police in Buenaventura. And I have come to fight on your side.'

Every word they spoke during a long conversation revealed one miracle after another. They threw themselves with all their souls into exchanging accounts of their experiences; their tongues wagged, their eyes sparkled, their ears drank in what they heard. Nor were the pleasures of the table neglected during the long wait to be able to speak to the Regional Governor. And this is what the Commandant told his dear friend, Babe.

15

How it happened that Babe killed Madonna-Jo's brother.

'The day will live for ever in my memory when I saw my mother and father killed and my sister raped. When the gang had withdrawn, there was no sign of my lovely sister. My parents, myself, the live-in butler and his wife and three little children were all taken to the local hospital and put in the morgue. As my father was registered as a Catholic, a priest was sent for to perform the necessary ceremonies over our corpses. Some of the holy water dripped into my eye and it seems I blinked. The priest noticed this and, checking, found there was still a pulse. To cut a long story short, in three weeks I was fit and able to interact with my fellows at the orphanage. You are aware, young friend, of what a pretty child I was. I grew ever more handsome. Father Croust, the priest in charge, became a most tender friend to me. He said I should train for the priesthood and in due course I was sent to Rome for training. The Father-General of the Order had requested young English novices. It appears the brethren running the Columbian diocese prefer non-Spanish speakers who are less likely to be influenced by the native peoples. Those least likely to be interested in attempting to converse in Spanish are the English. I was judged suitable by the Reverend Father to come and labour in this vineyard. Upon my arrival I was immediately appointed sub-deacon in the Church. In order to get closer to the people I found it expedient to ally myself with the local branch of the *Farc*. I soon achieved the rank of lieutenant. Today I am a fully fledged priest and a Colonel. We are vigorous in defending ourselves and the blessed poor against the capitalist imperialists. I am responsible for seeing to it that these are deprived of their possessions and put to death. It's brilliant that you have come to help us. But is it true that Madonna-Jo is in the area, at the home of the Chief of Police in Buenaventura?'

Babe swore to him that he had never spoken a truer word. More tears of joy were shed. The Colonel/Priest could not stop hugging Babe. He called him his brother, his salvation.

'Ah, it may be,' he said, 'that we shall be able to march together victorious into the city and find and rescue my dear sister!'

'Such is my dearest wish,' said Babe. 'She and I are engaged to be married, and then we can be ...'

'You insolent puppy!' the other interrupted. 'You expect to marry my sister, the daughter of a multi-millionaire! You've got a nerve, penniless as you are, to even think of such a thing. I bet you can't even afford a single Rolex!'

Babe stuttered, 'But, my good Sir, wealth and celebrity are not everything. I rescued your sister from the grasps of a media tycoon and an oligarch: she owes me. And anyway, she wants to marry me. Fabio said that all are equal who possess the necessary social skills and dress-sense, and I promise you I *shall* marry her!'

'We'll see about that, you villain!' roared Sir Harry Thunder-Smith, and so saying, he swung his swagger stick and caught Babe on the side of the head. Babe staggered, but recovered instantly, pulled out his knife, and thrust it to the hilt into the chest of the Colonel/Priest. Even as he withdrew it dripping with blood his tears were starting to flow, but not this time tears of joy.

'Oh crikey,' he said, 'I've killed my old friend, the son of my benefactor who brought me up, my intended brother-in-law. I'm the best-hearted man in the world, yet that's three men I've killed and all of them of high rank in society.'

Wayne, who had posted himself by the door, darted over.

'All we can do now is sell our lives dearly,' Babe told him. 'No doubt we'll be attacked at any moment. Be prepared!'

Wayne, who was not new to situations like this, kept his wits about him. He tore the uniform from the corpse, put it on Babe, put the distinctive hat on his head and pushed him towards the motorbikes. 'Let's burn some rubber, son! They'll think you're an officer on an urgent mission, we'll be out of reach before any pursuit starts.' Barely had he finished speaking than he was roaring off down the track, shouting in Spanish, 'Mind your backs! Make way for the Holy Commandant!'

16

*What became of the two travellers when they
met two girls, two monkeys and some wild
men called Mumps.*

Babe and his buddy were well clear of the outer limits of
the camp before the body of the English Colonel/Priest
was discovered. Wayne, ever resourceful, had ensured
their luggage was supplied with chocolate, ham, fruit and
some wine. They drove their trusty bikes off the beaten
track and into the wilderness. After a time they found
themselves crossing a wide stretch of open grassland criss-
crossed by small streams. They decided to rest and
consider. Wayne suggested they should have something to
eat whilst they were stopped. No sooner said than done –
on his part at least.

But: 'Do you really expect me,' said Babe, 'to tuck into
ham when I've just killed my benefactor's son and can
never expect ever to see my Madonna-Jo again? What is
the point of sustaining myself now when I'm doomed to a
life of misery and remorse far from the one I love? And
what will the *Guardian* be saying about it all?'

Even as he spoke he was managing to swallow his food.

The sun was beginning to set. The two travellers became
aware of hearing girlish cries. The sounds could have been
ones of pleasure or of pain, it was impossible to be sure,
but as travellers in a strange land the two men sprang
nervously to their feet. The noise came from two girls,

stark naked, who were running along the edge of the meadowland followed by two monkeys which appeared to be nipping at their bottoms with their teeth. Babe's heart-strings were tugged with pity at the sight. Amongst the Hackney Family he had been accredited as a sharpshooter who could take the lady off the bonnet of a Roller at three hundred yards without spoiling the paintwork. Now, two shots and both apes lay dead.

'Hurrah! How about that, young Wayne! I've saved those two poor girls from real danger: that makes up at least for my killing the oligarch and the tycoon. There's always the chance that those two are of a good family, and we might gain great profit from this in local society.'

He had been going to say more, but what he saw next choked the words off on his lips. The two girls flung themselves sobbing on the corpses of the apes and rent the air with loud lamentation.

'I thought they might be of good families,' said Babe eventually to Wayne, 'but I didn't expect such high standards of compassion and sensibility.'

Wayne replied ruefully, 'Oh well done my hero! All you've been and gone and done is to kill the two ladies' lovers.'

'Their lovers? You're having a laugh, Wayne. Do you really expect me to believe that?'

'Get real,' said Wayne. 'Everything seems to take you by surprise. You're not at home now. Why should you find it so surprising that there are countries where women fall in love with their genetic originators, the apes?'

'Blimey!' said Babe. 'I do remember Fabio telling me stories of things like that happening in antiquity, and of such couplings producing satyrs and similar strange offspring. But I thought evolution had taken us beyond that.'

'Well, now you know different,' retorted Wayne. 'Now

you know what un-evolved peoples are like. I just hope the two young ladies do not get us into hot water.'

These very reasonable reflections persuaded Babe that they should leave the open grassland and conceal themselves in the forest. There he and Wayne had something to eat, and, having both at length verbally consigned the media tycoon, the Chief of Police and the Colonel/Priest to the torments of hell, they fell asleep on a mossy bed. Waking up they found themselves immobilised. The reason, they discovered, was that during the night they had been tracked down by Mumps, as the local inhabitants were called, to whom the two girls had complained. The Mumps had bound them hand and foot with ropes made of fibre from the bark of the surrounding trees. They found themselves surrounded by fifty or so stark naked Mumps, all armed with arrows, clubs and stone axes. Some of them were tending the fire under a large cauldron, whilst others were preparing long skewers. All were chanting: 'Christians, Christians, vengeance and a good meal. Christians for dinner, Christians for dinner.'

'I told you I reckoned those girls would get us into hot water,' roared Wayne bitterly.

Babe looked at the cauldron and the skewers and lamented, 'We're either going to be boiled or spit-roasted. Oh, what would Fabio say at this spectacle of un-evolved humanity? OK, they've got only a very small carbon footprint, but I do think I'm hard done by to have lost my Madonna-Jo *and* to be spit-roasted by Mumps!'

Wayne never for a moment lost his head. 'Nil desperandum,' he said to an amazed Babe. 'I've picked up a bit of the local language. I'll try to talk to them.'

'Make sure they are well aware,' said Babe, 'what a primitive thing it is to cook other humans, and how uncivilised.'

'So,' said Wayne, 'you gentlemen are looking forward to

53

eating a Christian. Fair enough. Natural justice demands such treatment for your enemies. The law of the survival of the fittest teaches us to kill those around us and that's the way of the world. Where I live we don't exercise our right to eat our enemy, but that is only because we have plenty of other food. You are not so well provided for as we are: it's a shameful waste of a resource to abandon your enemies to the vultures and hyenas rather than recycling them. But, my good sirs, eating us, your friends, is not such a good idea. This is no Christian you are planning to roast, this is one of your defenders, the enemy of your enemies. Myself, I was born locally. Not only is my friend not a Christian, he's just killed one; it's his victim's clothes he's wearing. Truly, you shouldn't hate him. You can check I'm telling you the truth: take his jacket to the nearest checkpoint and ask if my friend has not just killed a priest. It won't take long and you can still eat us if you find I've lied. But if you find I've told you the truth, I'm sure you are too well versed in the principles and practice of natural law and the customs of the jungle not to spare us.'

The Mumps were most impressed by the quality of Wayne's exposition of the situation. They sent the sons of two elders to establish the facts with all due diligence. The two youngsters carried out their task enthusiastically and in no time at all they were back with the good news. The Mumps untied their prisoners, lavished all kinds of good treatment on them, offered them girls, gave them refreshments, and conducted them safely to their borders chanting: 'They're no Christians, they're no Christians.'

Babe could not get over the way he'd been treated. 'What a people!' he enthused. 'What real men! What manners! Just think, if I hadn't been lucky enough to find Madonna-Jo's brother's heart with my knife, I'd have been eaten by now. But at the end of the day, you can't beat uncivilised people: once they knew I wasn't a Christian they treated me superbly!'

17

*The arrival of Babe and Wayne in Eldorado,
and what they saw there.*

When they got to the Mumps' border: 'I think we can bear
witness,' said Wayne to Babe, 'that human nature in the
Southern Hemisphere is no better than in the Northern.
Let's get real: let's go back to the world we came from and
no mucking about.'

'But how can we?' said Babe. 'Our own country is
nothing but gangs and riots; in America I'd face the
electric chair. OK, stay here and we're likely to be spit-
roasted at any moment, but how can you expect me to
leave the part of the world that houses Madonna-Jo?'

'Let's head towards Cayenne,' was Wayne's suggestion.
'That's part of France. We'll find help there and proper
civilisation.'

It wasn't easy to get to Cayenne though. They knew
roughly which direction to go in, but they faced
overcoming terrible obstacles: mountains, rivers, canyons,
terrorists, natives. Almost immediately they had to
abandon their bikes for want of fuel and their sat-navs
packed up immediately afterwards because there was no
signal. They exhausted their provisions and lived for a
month on nothing but berries until they came to a stream
lined with palms and were able to revive their bodies and
souls with coconuts.

Wayne, whose advice Babe was finding as reasonable as

the old lady's, said, 'We're exhausted, we cannot go any further on foot. I've spotted a boat abandoned by the bank there. Let's pinch it. We'll fill it with coconuts, then just jump in and let the current take us where it will. Rivers always have people living near them; sooner or later we'll come to some kind of town. If we don't like what we find, tough – at least we'll have made progress of some sort.'

'Let's go!' said Babe. 'We'll take a chance on it.'

They drifted many miles through constantly changing scenery, the banks now bright with flowers, now bare and desert-like; flat one moment, steep cliffs the next. The river grew steadily bigger. Then it entered a narrow gorge where they could not see the tops of the cliffs towering up on either side. The two travellers held their breaths and consigned themselves to the rapids, finding themselves whirled along at a terrifying speed and in an overwhelming din. This went on for a whole twenty-four hours before the horizon opened out. But now, at the last moment, their boat shattered on a reef. Flung into the water they were obliged to struggle from rock to rock. At last the valley flattened out somewhat, though towering mountains could still be seen not far away, and the banks remained too steep to be negotiated. They became aware of cultivation, but it appeared driven as much by pleasure as by necessity. The fierceness of the sun seemed here to be pleasantly moderated in some way and plants were thriving. They could see roads with a good deal of traffic on them, but the coupés and cabriolets they saw all ran in total silence; they were certainly not diesel powered though they had the magnificence of the best 4x4s. Their drivers and passengers were strikingly good-looking: not one would have looked out of place pictured in *Country Life*.

'Blimey!' exclaimed Babe. 'This place looks even better than Surrey.'

They got on to the bank at the first village they came to. Some village children, wearing tattered garments of golden lace, were playing a kind of hockey at the bottom of the town walls. Our two friends from the civilised world enjoyed standing for a few minutes and watching them play. The stones they were using as pucks were quite large and metallic looking, and emitted a curious sound when struck. The two travellers were sufficiently intrigued to pick up a couple of them to inspect and found they were actually gold, platinum or rough diamonds. The smallest of them would not have looked out of place decorating the arm of a footballer's girlfriend.

'These kids,' opined Wayne, 'must be the offspring of some local popstar.'

At that moment the teacher from the school came to summon the children back into class. 'That must be the tutor they've employed,' reasoned Babe.

The little urchins abandoned their game when summoned and trotted off, leaving their sticks and stones lying where they were. Babe picked them up, ran after the teacher and tendered the stones to him with all due deference, trying to explain with signs that his honoured pupils had forgotten their precious trinkets. The teacher smiled, looked Babe in the face with some surprise, and threw them back on the ground before going into the school. You may be sure the travellers wasted no time in retrieving the gold, platinum and diamonds.

'Where can we be?' wondered Babe. 'These children must be incredibly well brought up to scorn in that way bling of such value.'

Wayne was just as surprised as Babe. Eventually they continued on their way towards the first house in the village itself. It was the size of a Texan ranch-house. They found a crowd of people outside the door and inside. Pleasant music was to be heard and delicious smells of cooking wafted out. Wayne went nearer to the crowd and could hear that they were speaking a Peruvian form of Spanish. His father had been a Peruvian footballer of some promise who had gone to Llanelli in the hope of a glittering career but, discovering that Llanelli was famous for the wrong kind of football, had ended up as a plasterer in Cardiff.

'I'll interpret for us,' he said. 'Let's go in, it's a kind of pub.'

At once two waiters and two waitresses, all dressed in gold cloth and their hair braided with gold filaments, showed them to a table and recommended the set menu of the day. They were served two bowls of consommé, each garnished with two macaws, a boiled condor which must have weighed a hundred kilos, two very flavoursome roast monkeys, one dish of three hundred humming-birds and another of six hundred guinea-fowl, various delicious stews and finally some exquisite pastries. The serving dishes were made of some kind of rock crystal. The waiters and waitresses plied them with various drinks made from sugar-cane.

Their fellow diners were for the most part shopkeepers and lorry drivers, all extremely polite, who asked questions of Wayne in the most tactful way imaginable and answered his with great civility.

When they had finished eating, Wayne, and indeed Babe, thought the right thing to do was to pay for it by putting on the table two of the pieces of gold they had picked up earlier. The landlord and his wife nearly split their sides laughing. Eventually they were able to speak.

'My dear gentlemen,' said the landlord, 'it is clear that you are strangers in our land. We never usually have visitors. You will please excuse our laughter at your trying to pay us with stones picked up off the street. You probably don't have any of the local currency, but you don't need it anyway to eat here. All inns intended to facilitate trade are fully subsidised by the Government. Ours is only a poor village, so I'm afraid we couldn't offer you anything much: elsewhere no doubt you will be offered something closer to what you are used to.'

Wayne explained to Babe what the landlord was saying; and Wayne in telling it and Babe in hearing it were both equally amazed and bewildered. What country was this, they wondered, cut off from the rest of the world and so very different from any other they had known? It was obviously a land where humans had evolved to a state of near perfection. Clearly such a place had to exist. And, whatever Fabio said, that place was definitely not Notting Hill.

18

What they saw in Eldorado.

Wayne owned to the landlord how curious they found it all. The landlord responded that he personally was pretty ignorant and didn't mind admitting it, but that he could introduce them to an elderly journalist who passed as being the most well-informed person in the country and who enjoyed talking about what he knew. He took Wayne straight round to meet the old man and Babe tagged along. They found themselves in a very simple cottage where the doors were made entirely of silver and the walls panelled entirely with gold, wrought with such loving care that they seemed the acme of the goldsmith's art. It was true that in the entrance hall the decorations were only of rubies and emeralds, but the artistry with which they were deployed made up for the cheapness of the materials.

The elderly gentleman greeted them sitting on a sofa stuffed with parrot feathers and offered them refreshments from beakers made of platinum. Once they were settled, he set about endeavouring to satisfy their curiosity as follows:

'I am one hundred and seventy-two years of age, and I learnt at my father's knee of the amazing revolutionary events in Peru which his father had witnessed as a child. You are in the former heartlands of the Inca Empire, from which its armies injudiciously sallied forth in search of lands to conquer. It was as a result of this that they were themselves liquidated by the Spanish. The leaders of the nation who had remained behind here in their fortress homeland learned their lesson: they decreed, and were supported in their decision by the whole of their people, that no inhabitant of the country should ever in future set foot outside of it. This has enabled us to preserve our innocent and contented way of life. The Spanish had some notion of the existence of the country and called it *El Dorado*. And later there was an Englishman called, I think, Thomas Cook, who came quite close to it at one time, but was deterred by the difficulties of crossing the mountains and chasms which guard us. Thus we have been protected from the ravening hoards of Europeans who might otherwise have descended upon our land, both to gasp at it in wondering admiration and to destroy it with mines and hotels, driving us into slavery, or death by disease.'

A long conversation ensued taking in forms of government, manners, feminism, the arts and the theatre. Babe, who – perhaps because of his Catholic adoptive father's interest in female vicars – was always inclined to be of a somewhat metaphysical turn of mind, asked through Wayne whether the country allowed any religion.

The old man flushed slightly. 'What's that?' he said. 'What do you take us for? Do you think we are not grateful for our good fortune?'

Wayne asked diffidently which religion was dominant in Eldorado. The old gentleman reddened again.

'Is there more than one religion? As far as I know our religion is that of the rest of the world: to worship our God morning, noon and night.'

'But do you worship only one god?' asked Wayne, who was good at guessing the questions Babe would want to ask.

'Obviously,' said the old man. 'How ever many are there supposed to be? You people do ask peculiar questions.'

Babe, though, was not deterred: he wanted to know what form their prayers took in Eldorado.

'We do not pray as such,' said the good and wise old man. 'We have nothing to ask of Him. He has provided us with all we could ask for; we have only to thank Him, which we never cease to do.'

Babe expressed a wish to meet some priests and asked where he might find them. The good old man smiled.

'My dear boys,' he said, 'we are all priests. From our President down, the head of every family performs the daily ritual of the morning thanksgiving.'

'Are there really no priests to lead you, to argue over what guidance to give you, to set up rival churches at the slightest sign of dispute?'

'We should be mad to want that,' said the old man. 'We all think the same way. What would we want with your priests?'

Babe was over the moon at all he was seeing and hearing. He said to himself: 'All this is very different from Notting Hill and Sir Digby and his vicar. If good old Fabio had been able to see this he would have had to revise his opinion as to the pre-eminence of Notting Hill society. Travel really does broaden the mind.'

To conclude their conversation the old man courteously asked his carer to take them in his silver solar-powered car to meet the President.

'Please excuse me,' he said, 'if I do not come with you. Old age has rather caught up with me. I'm sure you will be most graciously received. If you should find yourself uncomfortable with any of our customs, please excuse them for they are well-meant.'

Babe and Wayne settled into the incredible comfort of the vehicle and were whisked in luxurious silence to the Presidential Palace on the outskirts of the capital city. The entrance gate of the palace grounds was enormous and unbelievably ornate. Its decoration made what we call 'state-of-the-art ornamentation' look like pebble-dash.

Upon alighting, Babe and Wayne were welcomed by twenty gorgeous cheerleaders who took them straight to the sauna and dressed them in ceremonial robes made of down from hummingbirds. They were then conducted in procession by an officer bearing a platinum rod and accompanied by a five-hundred-piece marching band, as is the custom on these occasions. As they approached the President's receiving room, Wayne asked how they should greet and address him: whether they should bow from the waist or from the neck and how many times, whether they should put their hands on their hearts or behind their backs, or whether perhaps they were supposed to prostrate themselves.

'The custom,' replied the officer, 'is to shake hands and give him a kiss on each cheek.'

Babe and Wayne flung themselves on the President's neck and he received them with the utmost courtesy, inviting them to join him in a meal.

While this was being prepared he personally took them on a guided tour of the city, showing them the skyscrapers, the palatial shopping malls, the fountains running with pink water or with a sugar-cane drink, the magnificent squares paved with some material which seemed to give off scents of cinnamon and cloves. The President explained about the gauze they had developed and contrived to extend across the whole of the country from fixings on the mountain sides via the tops of all the high buildings, and which allowed rain through whilst moderating the effects of the sun. Babe asked to see the Law Courts, but was told there was no such thing as a law suit. He asked about prisons, and was told there was no need for them either. He was unable to see a hospital as there was no need of one: diseases had been eradicated and people died peacefully in their homes at an average age of 179. Babe was, though, greatly impressed by the 'Gallery of Science', a huge space celebrating the achievements of the country's scientists and engineers, not least the development of the gauze which, as well as improving the climate, obscured their cities from any prying eyes on the mountain-tops or in the skies.

At the end of the afternoon they had still been able to see only the smallest fraction of the city's wonders. They were taken back to the Presidential Palace and, along with several ladies, sat down to table with the President. They were regaled with the best meal they had ever eaten, more than worthy of a TV chef at home and the conversation sparkled, the President's wit losing none of its incisiveness by having to be translated by Wayne. Babe couldn't get over it.

They stayed a month in this luxurious accommodation. But Babe was constantly remarking to Wayne: 'I fully accept that the home I grew up in is no kind of a match for the merest hovel here. But I still miss Madonna-Jo and no doubt you have a girlfriend tucked away somewhere. If we stay here we are in no way superior to anyone else around, whereas if we go back to Europe and take just what we can carry in pebbles from here, we shall be rich enough to fear nothing and no-one, and will easily be able to recover Madonna-Jo.'

Wayne could not disagree. There is so much pleasure to be had, after one has travelled, in gaining prestige by recounting one's adventures that the two men decided to forego their good fortune and to take their leave of the President.

'I think you are being stupid,' the President told them bluntly. 'I know my country is nothing special, but when you find somewhere you can be reasonably well contented, I think it's best to stay there. Clearly I have no right to forbid you to leave: such a tyranny would be foreign to us. All men are free. If you must go, go. But I have to advise you that leaving the country is a major undertaking. There is no way you can fight your way back up the river you were swept down. The mountains surrounding us are twelve thousand feet high and fall sheer on our side. However, I'll put my scientists to work on building a machine to hoist you up the side of the mountain – we do not allow the development of flying machines, having no wish to leave our land. You will be transported to the top of the mountains, but no-one will be able to go with you to make sure that you are safe: my people have vowed never to leave the sanctuary of their homeland and they are too sensible to want to break their vow. I also have to remind you that this will be an experimental machine, and there is no question of offering you any insurance. Now tell me, is there anything more you wish from me?'

'Only,' said Wayne, 'a few bags of provisions and some of the country's pebbles and dust.'

The President laughed. 'It is beyond me what you Europeans see in our yellow and grey soil. Take as much as you want, and much good may it do you.'

He gave his orders and three thousand scientists and engineers worked round the clock. In a fortnight all the development work had been done and the machine was ready. The cost was the equivalent of no more than four million euros in local currency.

Babe and Wayne climbed on to the machine. They were accompanied by any number of solar-powered shopping trolleys laden with provisions, with gifts of local specialities, and with gold, diamonds, platinum and other rare metals. The President took fond leave of his 'tramps', as he called them.

Their departure was spectacular and in no time they

found themselves deposited safely on the summit of one of the mountains.

Babe's only thought now was of Madonna-Jo. 'We'll be able to buy her freedom from the Chief of Police, if he can only be persuaded to put a value on her. Let's head towards Cayenne. From there we'll look around for a country to buy!'

19

*What befell them in Guiana, and how Babe
made the acquaintance of Martin.*

Our two travellers quite enjoyed the first day of their trek.
The idea of their being the richest men in the world took
their minds off any hardships. Babe in his excitement
carved Madonna-Jo's name on tree trunks as they went
along. During the second day two of their trolleys became
bogged down and had to be abandoned. A few days later
the solar engines on two more trolleys stopped working,
and then their passage through a particularly dark stretch
of forest accounted for several more. As time went on,
others ran out of control and were lost over cliffs. By the
time they reached the hundredth day of their journey, only
two were left to them.

Babe was minded to moralise to Wayne: 'You see how
impermanent worldly goods are: the only things that are
imperishable are good-nature and the joy of seeing
Madonna-Jo.'

'No doubt,' responded Wayne, 'but the fact still
remains that in the two remaining trolleys we have more
wealth than anyone on the *Sunday Times* rich list, and in
the distance I can see a town which I think must be in
Guiana. We are near the end of our travails. Happiness is
at hand.'

Just short of the edge of the town they came across a
young man lying by the side of the road, wearing only a

pair of denim shorts. The poor man had lost his left leg and his right hand.

'Good Lord!' said Babe to him. 'Whatever are you doing here in this condition?'

'I'm waiting for my scientists,' replied the boy.

'Did they do this to you?'

'Oh yes, and this is all the clothes we're given to wear. When we're testing drugs, if a finger becomes gangrenous they chop off a hand and if we try to run away they chop off a leg. Both have happened to me. That's why medicines are so expensive. Yet when my widowed mother sent me off in the hope I would be able to send back enough money to support her and my baby sisters, she told me to be sure to pray regularly to the saint she hung around my neck and I would be sure of happiness and prosperity. It doesn't seem to have worked: dogs, monkeys and parrots are better treated than we are. They keep telling us that we are benefiting mankind. I don't know what you think, but speaking as a man, I can't say I feel the benefit.'

'Oh Fabio!' exclaimed Babe. 'You failed to teach me that such abominations are possible in the name of scientific progress. That does it! I no longer believe in inexorable progress!'

'What do you mean by that?' asked Wayne.

'Oh,' sighed Babe, 'it is the madness of thinking that the world is in the process of evolving towards a possible future perfection.' He shed tears over the poor boy at the roadside and his cheeks were still wet as they entered the town.

First of all they enquired about the possibilities of travelling by road to Buonaventura – they felt they couldn't consider flying with the two trolleys. A French travel agent thought he could offer them a good deal; he said he would make some enquiries and they arranged to meet him again in a restaurant to conclude the bargain.

Babe and his faithful friend Wayne duly turned up at the restaurant.

Babe, who was prone to wear his heart on his sleeve, told the Frenchman all that had happened to them and affirmed his intention of recovering Madonna-Jo.

'There's no way I'm going to get involved in helping you make it to Buonaventura,' said the agent. 'My rep. would hang for it and so would you. I've read in the gossip columns that your Madonna-Jo is considered the favourite mistress of the Chief of Police.'

Poor Babe was heart-broken.

When he had recovered his senses somewhat he drew Wayne to one side. 'Here's what I'm going to ask you to do for me as my friend. We've both got in our pockets millions of pounds worth of diamonds. You are more cunning than I am. You go and get Madonna-Jo out of Buonaventura for me. If the Chief of Police makes things awkward, offer him a million. If that's not enough, offer him two million. You haven't killed any media tycoons, you'll be safe enough. I'll find a way of getting to Zurich and I'll wait for you to join me there. Switzerland is a free country, where there's nothing to fear from gangs or oligarchs or media tycoons, and where we can hide our wealth with no questions asked.'

Wayne considered this an excellent idea. He hated the thought of being separated from his good friend, but consoled himself with the belief that he was doing him a great service. They took an emotional farewell of each other. Babe urged him not to forget to bring the old lady out too. Wayne left the same day: he was truly a good-hearted man.

Babe stayed on a bit longer in French Guiana, trying to find the best way to smuggle himself and his two trolleys into Switzerland. Finally, he came across a certain Mr Vanderdendur from neighbouring Surinam who claimed to have the necessary transport and contacts.

'How much,' Babe asked him, 'would I have to pay for you to get me, one companion, and my two shopping trolleys into Zurich without the authorities noticing?' The gentleman quoted a round one million euros; Babe did not hesitate.

'Hey up!' said Mr Vanderdendur to himself. 'He doesn't blink at offering a million just like that; he must be absolutely rolling in it.'

He returned to Babe a few minutes later having 'made a phone call' and said he would actually require two million. 'So be it,' said Babe.

'By the left,' thought Mr Vanderdendur, 'this chap coughs up two million as readily as one!'

Another 'consultation with his contacts' and he came back with the news that it would take three million to get him into Zurich unseen. 'OK,' said Babe, 'three million it is.'

'Well, well!' said the facilitator to himself. 'This bloke is indifferent to paying three million. There must be something incredibly valuable in those two weird trolley things. Best not to push it any further. Let's get our hands on the three million, then we'll see.'

Babe sold two diamonds, getting for them more than twice what he owed the Dutchman. He paid up. A truck took the two trolleys out to the plane and they were put in the hold. Babe started to walk across the field to the aircraft; it revved its engines, taxied unhurriedly to the far end of the field and took off. Babe, aghast and amazed, soon lost it from view.

'Oh ****!' he screamed. 'If that isn't a trick worthy of a European!'

He made his way back into town utterly dispirited at the loss of enough money to buy up the whole of the English Premier League.

Babe betook himself to Police Headquarters. Being

71

rather upset he was inclined to shout about what had happened to him and to bang the counter. He suffered a spot fine of one thousand euros for disturbing the peace. The policeman then listened properly and promised to investigate, but only after making it clear that a down payment of a further thousand euros would 'enable adequate resources to be found'.

Babe was plunged into the uttermost depths of despair. In reality this was not by any means the worst of the troubles he had encountered, but the dishonest conduct of the Dutchman and of the policeman enveloped him in a black depression. Human depravity presented itself to his mind in all its ugliness, and melancholy assailed him. Eventually, he identified a container ship heading for Bordeaux which had cabins for a handful of passengers and whose agent agreed to take him. Feeling in need of a companion with whom to share the long voyage, he advertised in the town for an honest man who would be willing to travel with him, to have his passage and board paid and to receive a fee of twenty thousand euros. The only condition he made was that the man he chose would be the one who was most disgusted and miserable at the state of the world in which he found himself and at his own way of life.

As it turned out the swarm of applicants who presented themselves could not have been accommodated on the largest cruise ship. Babe tried to pick out the most likely candidates, and whittled it down to twenty men who seemed reasonably pleasant company and who had some claim to meet the conditions he had laid down. He brought them together in a restaurant, bought them a meal and put them on oath to give a true account of themselves. For his part he promised to pick the one who seemed the most deserving of pity and the most entitled to feel himself to be at the nadir of misery; the others would receive some recompense for their trouble in applying.

The proceedings went on until four in the morning. Babe, listening to their stories, was often reminded of what Madonna-Jo's companion had said during the voyage to Buonaventura and of her wager that they would find no-one on board who had not suffered terrible hardship. With each tale he heard he thought also of Fabio. 'Dear old Fabio,' he thought to himself, 'would be very hard pressed to show how this fitted in with his view of the world. I wish he were here. It really seems that it is only in Eldorado that human life approaches perfection, nowhere else.' In the end he chose a down-at-heel computer scientist who had spent ten years working in Seattle. It seemed impossible to imagine a more degraded way of life than the one he now had.

This boffin, who was actually a really good and decent man, had been made redundant, stripped of his possessions by his wife, beaten up by his son, and had his daughter walk out on him to elope with a Mexican. He had been forced to flee persecution in the USA because he had been spotted reading a tattered copy of *The God Delusion* which he had retrieved from a bin. In Guiana he'd just lost the menial part-time job from which he'd been feeding himself. In actual fact the other nineteen were probably equally badly off, but Babe thought him the most intelligent of them and the most likely to be good company. The others all reckoned themselves extremely hard done by, but felt a little better upon the gift of a thousand euros each.

20

What happened to Babe and Martin during their journey by sea.

So the scientist, whose name was Martin, and Babe boarded the container ship bound for Bordeaux. Both men had seen and endured much: if they'd been embarking on a voyage around the world they would have had enough material for discussion never to have felt the time long. Babe had one great advantage over Martin, which was that he travelled in the hope of seeing Madonna-Jo again, whereas Martin had nothing to hope for. Furthermore, Babe had pockets full of gold and diamonds; true he had lost a hundred times that fortune, true the dishonesty of the Dutch facilitator still sickened him when he thought of it; but when he considered what he still had, and when – perhaps at the end of a good meal – he spoke of Madonna-Jo, then he thought that, conceivably, Fabio was not so far wrong in his rosy view of the world.

'And what about you, Martin?' he asked the scientist. 'What do you think about the perfectibility of the human race? Are we evolving steadily towards moral and physical perfection?'

'Sir,' replied Martin, 'I was accused in the USA of being an atheist; the truth is that I am a Satanist.'

'You're kidding me,' said Babe. 'Nobody's a Satanist nowadays.'

'Well, I am,' asserted Martin. 'I'm sorry, but that is how I see it.'

'Are you saying that you have been taken over by the Devil?'

'I see his hand in so many aspects of the world,' said Martin, 'that I have no reason to suppose that he's not in me. If I look around this world, this little sphere of matter wandering through space, I can only conclude that it is under the control of some evil spirit – all of it except Eldorado, of course. Every individual, every community, every nation, is trying to gain advantage by standing on the body of its neighbour. Those at the bottom of the pile loath and abominate those who have cheated their way to the top; and those at the top despise and exploit those below them. Throughout the Western world businessmen, bankers, media-men, politicians, all enrich themselves with power and wealth by exploiting the frailties of those less ruthless than themselves. Every city is riddled with the disease of envy; not just of the poor for the wealthy, but of those less well educated for those who have more qualifications; the envy of those who understand little of 'high' culture for those who understand more; the envy of those who have never travelled for those who have seen something of the world, however superficially. Suppressed private jealousies are actually more debilitating than public ills. At the end of the day, everything I have seen and suffered has made me believe in the power of Satan.'

'And yet good does exist,' said Babe.

'If you say so,' replied Martin, 'but I've yet to encounter it.'

In the midst of their debate they heard the sound of an aircraft's engines. The word spread rapidly round the ship that the plane was broadcasting a Mayday message: apparently there was a man on board who appeared deranged and was threatening to explode a bomb if he was not allowed to parachute on to a nearby island with some of the plane's precious cargo. Suddenly, a flash of red was visible and the plane disintegrated in the air not far from the container ship.

'You see how men treat each other!' said Martin.

'It really does seem as though there is some devil at work,' said Babe.

The sea and nearby shore were littered with wreckage, and boats were put off to see if anything or anyone could be recovered. Imagine Babe's joy when, amongst the mangled corpses and odds and ends of suitcases, clothes and packing cases brought back to the ship, he recognised the distinctive shape of one of his high-tech trolleys which had miraculously survived intact. The plane had been the one carrying the riches stolen from Babe; the Dutch criminal was at the bottom of the sea with all his plunder, bar the one trolley.

'So you see,' Babe observed to Martin, 'sometimes crime is punished; that Dutch rogue got what he deserved.'

'True,' responded Martin. 'But what about the others on the plane who had to die with him?'

The ship resumed its voyage and the two men resumed their debate, but the latter made far less progress than the former. As they talked, however, Babe would feast his eyes upon his trolley, seeing it as perhaps an omen. 'If I've got this back,' he thought to himself, 'perhaps I can recover Madonna-Jo too.'

21

Still debating with each other, Babe and Martin approach the French coast.

After many days at sea, they sighted the French coast on the horizon. Have you spent much time in France?' asked Babe.

'Oh yes,' replied Martin. 'I worked for a computer repair company, going all over France repairing IT equipment. I didn't like the French. Half of them are mad, a lot are sneaky bastards, some of them seem to suffer from inbred stupidity, just a few have some wit. They all have in common that their first thought is always of the opposite sex, their second thought is to slander their rivals, and their third concern is to speak ill of Britain and Germany.'

'What did you think of Paris?'

'Not much. The main preoccupation there seems to be to rip off tourists. I didn't spend long there. My first evening I was mugged in a street in St Denis by two Arabs. When apprehended they accused me of attacking them for racial reasons and I spent a week in jail. I lost my job and had to work in a call-centre for a time to get together enough money for my fare home. The things I heard on those phones! The French claim to be lovers of their language and of their culture: it didn't sound much like it to me.'

'I'm not bothered about spending any time in France,' said Babe. 'Even if it was as wonderful as other people say it is, after a month in Eldorado, you know... All I want to see is Madonna-Jo. I'm going to wait for her in Zurich. Will you come with me?'

'Gladly,' said Martin. 'They say that the Swiss are very welcoming to visitors with money to spend. I haven't got any, so I'll be glad to follow you wherever you go.'

'By the way,' said Babe, 'have you come across the idea that fossil remains show that at one time the whole of Europe, including the Alps, lay under the ocean?'

'I think that's all nonsense,' replied Martin. 'People should look at the height of the mountains and believe the evidence of their own eyes.'

'So how did the world come to be as it is, with all the different strata of rocks and so on?'

'Satan moves in a mysterious way, his wonders to perform.'

Babe tried again: 'I told you about those two Mump girls who were in love with monkeys, didn't I? Doesn't that astonish you?'

'Not in the slightest,' replied Martin. 'I've seen so many weird things, nothing can astonish me any more.'

'Do you think humans have evolved to be as they are now, or have they always wanted ever-improved weapons with which to wipe each other out? Have they always been liars; deceitful, perfidious, ungrateful brigands; weak, fickle, cowardly, jealous, greedy, drunken, miserly, self-seeking, blood-thirsty, slanderous, debauched, fanatical, hypocritical and stupid?'

'Haven't hawks always eaten pigeons?'

'Presumably.'

'Well then,' pursued Martin, 'if hawks have always had the same genetic characteristics why should you think humans have changed?'

'But,' said Babe, 'there is the difference that humans have the power of reason...'

They were still debating when the ship arrived in Bordeaux.

22

How Babe and Martin got on in France.

Babe stopped in Bordeaux only long enough to sell a few of the pebbles from Eldorado. He also disposed of the trolley, which since its fall and dowsing in sea water had become an impediment, by donating it to the Faculty of Science at the university. There it was given to some doctorate students as a research project, and a year later a paper was published proving conclusively that the maximum power it could generate was not enough to turn its wheels.

Babe had intended to fly direct to Zurich, but since the only flights available involved changing in Paris, and since every inch of advertising space on the road out to the airport and in the terminal was given over to extolling the pleasures of a stay in the capital, Babe decided that perhaps it would be a waste not to spend a bit of time there. So, unable to forgo the companionship of his philosophical friend, he purchased two single tickets to Paris.

He took advantage of an incredible offer which packaged the airline tickets with rooms in a five-star hotel in Montmartre. When they arrived, Babe was not impressed with the look of the area – more Shepherds Bush than Notting Hill, he thought.

Even as Babe was checking in he suddenly felt unwell, his indisposition no doubt a consequence of the stress of the last few weeks. Since he was wearing a huge diamond on his finger and generally exuded wealth, a doctor was whistled up in no time by the hotel management, and before he knew where he was he was in a bedroom and all sorts of equipment was being wheeled in along with two nurses to look after it and him. This caused Martin to remark that on his first visit to Paris he had been taken ill as well, but being penniless he had had the greatest difficulty in securing the most rudimentary treatment from the local pharmacist.

The tranquillisers with which the doctor treated Babe seemed to make him worse rather than better. He was visited by an insurance salesman who wanted him to insure himself for funeral expenses. Babe tried to tell him to get lost, but the nurses assured him that such insurance was considered essential in the best Parisian society. Babe said he didn't belong to the best Parisian society. Martin tried to throw the salesman out of the window. The salesman swore that it would be impossible for anyone to bury Babe. Martin promised to bury the salesman if he carried on. Eventually, Martin literally kicked him out. Gradually, Babe's health improved. He had lots of company from other guests in the hotel and a regular poker school developed in his room. Babe was amazed that he never seemed to be dealt winning hands; Martin did not find it so surprising.

Once Babe was well enough to go out and about, the hotel offered to supply him with a personal Paris guide of impeccable credentials who would allow him to get to know the real Paris. The guide turned out to be from Marseilles originally, one of those slick Provençal types, ever alert and serviceable, smooth and ebullient, always on the look-out for tourists to whom he can offer pleasure and excitement to suit their pocket and their whim. First he took Babe and Martin to the theatre where a new musical was playing. Babe found himself sitting next to a supercilious chap who was quick to tell him that normally he only went to the opera. When Babe could not restrain a tear at a particularly moving scene, his neighbour informed him that the music was actually derivative and repetitive, that the singer's low register was very weak, the amplification tinny, and that the director's idea of an Arabian Casbah clearly showed he had never seen the real thing. Babe asked the guide how many musicals might be playing in France at that moment.

'Thirty or forty I expect,'

'How many of them are any good?'

'Three or four.'

'As many as that?' said Martin.

Babe was particularly struck by one of the actresses. 'I really like that girl,' he told Martin. 'Her looks remind me of Madonna-Jo. I'd quite like to meet her.'

The Provençal was doubtful whether even he could gain access to the star, whose name was Clarisse Clairon. Babe asked who the insensitive idiot was he had been sitting next to, who seemed so oblivious to the charms of the piece.

'Oh him,' said the guide. 'He's a kind of professional tweeter: he spends his time tweeting spiteful comments about everything and everyone, on the strength of which the so-called wit is invited to all the best parties, to appear on chat shows and write scurrilous articles for the weekend magazine supplements.'

Talking thus, Babe, Martin and the guide stood hesitating on the grand staircase of the theatre watching the audience disperse.

'Much as I am dying to find Madonna-Jo again,' sighed Babe, 'I really would like to meet that Clarisse Clairon. I did think she was so good.'

'I honestly do not think there's any chance of getting past her bodyguards,' said the guide, 'but where I am proposing to take you will give you every possibility of meeting the best that Parisian society has to offer.'

He took them to the home of a lady styling herself the

Marquise de Parolignac, in the Faubourg St Honoré. When they went in she was supervising games of pontoon. A dozen affluent-looking obese people with pale, serious faces sat in earnest and silent groups whilst the Marquise observed, taking in every wince, every attempted sleight of hand, every fleeting expression of triumph. Her daughter, about eighteen years old, was one of the players, winking at her mother to draw attention to the tricks of her fellows. The Marquise acted as banker, and her self-control and control of the players were absolute. When Babe and Martin were led in by the guide there was no reaction whatsoever from any of the pale faces absorbed in their cards and the Marquise barely looked a greeting. Even Lady Petal was more polite, thought Babe.

However, the guide went up to the Marquise and whispered in her ear. She deigned to smile at Babe and Martin, and showed Babe to a seat where she dealt him into a game. In the first two hands Babe lost fifty thousand euros. Everyone was amazed at how indifferent he appeared to his loss.

'Probably an English investment banker,' muttered the staff amongst themselves.

A buffet meal was served and it went as all such gatherings do: an uncomfortable silence was followed by a burst of noise such that one could hardly distinguish a word that was said; then insipid jokes, rumour, illogicality, a smattering of politics, a lot of bad-mouthing. Eventually, however, the inevitable question of a federal Europe arose.

'Did anyone read Cardinal Gauchet's piece about how Europe could become a reincarnation of the Holy Roman Empire?' asked someone.

'Humph!' responded one of the swells. 'There's just so much nonsense talked, I despair. That's why I come here and fritter my wealth away playing pontoon. There's no point in trying to hang on to it.'

'What about that article in *Le Monde* by that Norwegian neo-fascist?' asked the man from Marseilles.

'Oh, that rag disgusts me!' declared Mme de Parolignac. 'I do object to the way it offers extreme opinions so uncritically; it destroys the very case it is trying to make. I shall not be buying that paper any more.'

There was present one man who seemed more level-headed than the rest. He spoke of how nations could not expect continual growth in their economies, any more than any individual could expect without fail to spend their life getting steadily richer. He argued cogently that nations should see their long-term advantage to be in cooperating for the common good rather than seeking short-term advantage over their neighbours for the sake of prestige.

'It's all the fault of the party system of democracy,' he said, 'which encourages our representatives, who need to be re-elected every few years, to think only of what they can offer the voters over short periods and refuse far-sighted policies which might cause transient unpopularity. Furthermore, the party system dissuades people from using the powers of reason which they have evolved to enjoy: they prefer instead to trot out stale clichés, and rely on the thinking of the previous century when their party was first formed.'

Babe listened attentively to what this gentleman was saying and conceived the greatest respect for the speaker. He took the liberty of whispering in his hostess's ear to ask her who this was who expressed himself so admirably.

'He's a university lecturer,' was the reply. 'He never actually gambles, though he seems to enjoy the company here. He stands as an independent in every election that comes round, offering sensible and well-argued policies, but never receives more than a handful of votes.'

'He is a truly fine man,' mused Babe. 'He reminds me of Fabio.'

So Babe turned to him to say, 'You believe, I suppose, that given time and evolution mankind is capable of achieving perfection: that, as a friend of mine now unfortunately executed, put it, "the bad things we see around us are merely hiccoughs on the road to perfection."'

'I can't say I agree with that,' said the lecturer. 'It seems to me that people are pretty well set in their need to quarrel and dispute: left-wing with right-wing, climate-change believers with deniers, europhiles with europhobes, high tax economists with investment bankers and venture capitalists, women's libbers with their husbands, parents with their children: it's a battleground we live in.'

'Your executed friend,' interjected Martin, 'was having a laugh with his hiccoughs. Man causes as many disasters now as ever he did.'

Most of the gambling fraternity had no comprehension of the debate they were hearing and merely went on drinking. Martin and the lecturer continued in friendly argument, while Babe told his hostess something of his adventures.

A little later, the buffet being cleared and play resumed, the Marquise drew Babe into a side room and sat him down on the sofa next to her.

'So,' she began, 'you are hopelessly in love with Miss Thunder-Smith?'

'Indeed I am,' replied Babe.

The Marquise smiled enigmatically. 'That was the reply of a true Englishman. A Frenchman would have said: "I used to love her, but having seen you, lady, I feel my affections changing."'

'I'm so sorry,' stammered Babe. 'I'll give you any reply you wish.'

'I understand that you fell in love with her when she asked you for a Kleenex. Oh! Please would you pick up my handkerchief which I seem to have dropped.'

'With pleasure,' said Babe.

'And tuck it back into my bodice for me where I like to keep it.' Babe did as he was bidden. 'You see,' murmured the lady, 'I am favouring you on our first date because you are a foreigner. Sometimes I make men come on to me for a fortnight before I stop teasing them.'

The lady went on to lavish such praise on the two diamonds Babe was wearing on his fingers that in no time at all they were on hers.

Babe went back to the others feeling somewhat guilty that he had been unfaithful to Madonna-Jo. The city guide had no difficulty in guessing his state of mind; he was already intrigued by Babe's apparent indifference to the loss of fifty thousand euros and scented the possibility of profit for himself. He spoke to Babe at length on the subject of Madonna-Jo and Babe was moved to assure him that his first act upon meeting her in Zurich would be to ask her pardon for his infidelity.

The guide redoubled his attentiveness, taking a kind interest in all Babe's activities and plans. 'So, you have a *rendez-vous* to keep in Zurich.'

'Oh yes, my friend,' replied Babe. 'I really must find Madonna-Jo again.' And, as was his wont, he succumbed to the pleasure of speaking of his beloved and recounted yet again some part of his adventures with the beautiful young lady.

'I suppose,' ventured the guide, 'that your beloved sends you a constant stream of witty and affectionate emails.'

'I don't think she's got my phone number or my email address, any more than I have hers,' sighed Babe. 'The circumstances of our meetings and partings have made it impossible for us to keep in touch. All I could do was to send my good friend Wayne to try and seek her out.'

The guide listened carefully and thoughtfully, then he excused himself most politely and hoped they would enjoy the rest of their evening. The next morning the hotel receptionist handed over to Babe a message addressed to him:

My dearest darling, I've been here a week and I've been ill the whole time. Now I learn that you are in the same city! If only I was capable of rising from my bed I would fly into your arms. I heard that you came here via Bordeaux. That's where I've left Wayne and Tiffany who will follow on soon. The Chief of Police robbed me of everything I had, save only my love for you. Please come to me: seeing you I shall either recover or die of happiness.

This charming and most unexpected letter transported Babe to the very heights of ecstatic joy, whilst at the same time he was plunged into the depths of despair by the news of his beloved's illness. Torn between the two emotions he seized up his gold and his diamonds, grabbed Martin and a taxi, and hastened to the hotel where Madonna-Jo was staying. He entered her room trembling with excitement, his heart thumping, a sob in his voice, and made at once to draw back the curtains to allow him to see his young lady.

'No, no!' cried the nurse in attendance. 'You mustn't do that. The light could kill her.' And she brusquely pulled the curtains back together.

'My darling Madonna-Jo,' Babe stammered, 'how are you? If I cannot see you properly, at least let me hear you.'

'She cannot speak,' said the nurse.

Then the girl in the bed put her plump hand in Babe's, and Babe kissed it and covered it with his tears, and pressed into it a handful of diamonds before putting a bag full of gold dust on the bedside table.

Into this cauldron of emotion came thrusting the Provençal guide, followed by a man who *looked* official, though he wore no uniform. The latter immediately seized Babe by the arm, announcing that he was from the

Immigration Service and that Babe had entered the country illegally.

'I'm a bona fide traveller with a European passport but it's back at the hotel,' protested Babe. 'They didn't treat travellers like this in Eldorado,' he sighed to himself.

'I see again the hoof of Satan in this,' muttered Martin.

'Where are you taking me?' asked Babe.

'To a holding camp pending extradition proceedings,' said the official.

Quickly recovering from his surprise at these events, Martin realised that the lady claiming to be Madonna-Jo was an impostor, that the official might well be also but was certainly in league with the guide, and that the guide was a rascal who had seen an opportunity to take advantage of Babe's innocence. He whispered his conclusions to Babe who, aware that he had not declared his precious metals at Customs and anxious to risk no delay in seeing the real Madonna-Jo, decided not to make a fuss but to buy the three of them off with three little diamonds each.

'Oh!' exclaimed the official. 'Whatever crimes you have committed in entering the country, I see that you are a thoroughly honest man. Let me assist you to leave the country without going through Customs. It's easier at seaports than at airports. At airports they spend two to three hours X-raying and searching passengers in their most secret places. At seaports you simply have to flash your passport.'

Babe was disgusted. 'The sooner I get out of this ridiculous country and am on my way to Zurich, the better I'll like it,' he said.

'I can't get you into Zurich,' said the official, 'but with the help of my brother-in-law I can get you out through the port of Dieppe.'

In what seemed no time at all Babe and Martin were at

Dieppe and being handed over to the brother-in-law, who, with the gift of three more diamonds turned out to be as helpful as they come. He smuggled them on board a brand-new luxury yacht which, with a crew of only two, was being delivered to its owners in Italy. It was agreed that Babe and Martin would be dropped off in Bilbao, from where they could find a flight onward to Zurich.

23

Babe and Martin reach Spain: what they find there.

'Ah, Fabio, Fabio! Oh, Martin! Oh, my darling Madonna-Jo! What kind of a world is this we live in?' sighed Babe as they crossed the Bay of Biscay.

'A pretty mad and abominable one,' groaned Martin.

'You have some knowledge of Spain: are the people there as mad as those we met in France?'

'It's a different kind of madness,' replied Martin, 'which I believe in recent years has had rather different results.'

They sailed into the port of Bilbao. Half the population of the town seemed to be living in cardboard boxes on the quayside. At the sight of the luxury yacht they stood as one and howled and roared and shook their fists.

'Where are the police who might allow us to berth?' asked Babe.

'It appears,' said their captain, 'that the government cannot afford to pay policemen: there is no police force any more. The country is bankrupt.'

Indeed, looking beyond the port they could see that the buildings were either dilapidated or burnt, neglected or suffering from riot damage.

'But how have things been allowed to come to this pass?' asked Babe. 'Surely Spain's partners in Europe could help!'

'They could, but they won't,' replied Martin. 'They

think it is in their interests to allow Spain to disintegrate and fall into a state of anarchy and irredeemable poverty.'

'But why?'

'To encourage the others,' was the reply.

It was clearly not safe for anyone to try to land from the yacht. Eager as he was to get to Zurich as quickly as possible, Babe was so shocked and dumbfounded by the conditions in Spain that he was indifferent to the possibility of the captain's being another pirate and agreed to fork out more diamonds to stay on board as far as Genoa. From there they took the train to Zurich. It was with some emotion that Babe stepped out on to the platform at the station there. He embraced Martin: 'We've made it!' he said. 'Soon I shall see my lovely Madonna-Jo. I can trust Wayne as I trust myself. All is well, all will be well, all is right with the world!'

24

About Felicita, and about Herr Nelke.

As soon as he was settled in Zurich, Babe set about searching for Wayne in all the bars, all the cafés, all the nightclubs, but there was no sign of him. Every day he made enquiries at the station and the airport, but there was no news of Wayne.

'How can this be?' he complained to Martin. 'Think of the time it has taken me to get from Guiana to Bordeaux, on to Paris, across to Dieppe, down to Bilbao, round to Genoa and across to Zurich, and in all that time Madonna-Jo still has not arrived! Instead of her all I've found is a Paris guide from Provence and a Madonna-Jo impersonator. I think Madonna-Jo must be dead and I cannot conceive of my continuing to live. Oh, I should have stayed in the paradise that was Eldorado, not returned to this benighted Europe. You are so right, my friend: life is nothing but illusion and disaster.'

One day Babe was strolling by the lake, outwardly listening to Martin and inwardly longing for Madonna-Jo when his attention was drawn to a young man with a girl on his arm. The man, healthily plump and virile, strode out confidently, head held high. The girl was very pretty and sang to herself as she walked along. Every so often she would look lovingly at her companion and stroke his cheek.

'Admit it, those two at least are contented people,'

observed Babe to Martin. 'It's true that up to now, in all my travels other than in Eldorado, I have found nobody who was not discontented. But looking at that couple, I am willing to bet they are happy people.'

'I bet they're not,' said Martin.

'Let's invite them to have lunch with us,' said Babe. 'Then you'll see if I'm not right.'

Without further ado he accosted them and invited them to eat with him on the terrace of a nearby restaurant, where the set menu for lunch was a dish of local fresh partridge and truffles with rösti. The girl looked embarrassed, but the man, who turned out to be a teacher at a prestigious boarding school, accepted gracefully. As they walked to their table the girl looked at Babe with some surprise and confusion in her eyes, and indeed a hint of tears. The man excused himself and went off to find the loo, and hardly had they sat down than she addressed Babe:

'Oh dear! I recognise Mr Babe, but you do not recognise the Felicita you used to know!'

Babe had not looked properly at the girl until then, his mind being too full of thoughts of Madonna-Jo, but now: 'Good gracious is it really you! But you were the girl who was responsible for the fine state of health in which I found Fabio!'

'I'm afraid that may be true,' admitted Felicita. 'You obviously know all about it. I heard about the awful fate that befell Sir Digby's household and the lovely Madonna-Jo. I have to tell you, in all honesty, I have scarcely fared any better. I was quite an innocent when you knew me and all too easily seduced by one of my fellow countrymen, who was working as a designer in London, and who befriended me. It all led to my being kicked out of the house not long after you had felt the weight of Sir Digby's boot. A local chemist from whom I sought medicines helped me out and set me up in a flat. He was ugly as sin and I didn't like him, but there was nothing I could do, penniless, visa-less and miserable as I was. His wife found out about me and beat me half to death. He gave her what he said was a new cold-cure to try and she died in convulsions before they could get her to hospital. He disappeared and I was the one who ended up in a police cell. Fortunately, I still had my looks, and the legal-aid solicitor appointed to help me was easily persuaded to pull some strings and get me released. He brought me on holiday to Zurich, but soon found someone else and I was forced into becoming an escort girl to survive. I don't know if you can conceive of what it's like to be at the mercy of men of all kinds, from tour guides to tourists, from lawyers to priests; to be regularly insulted by those who think themselves better than you; to be reduced to having to borrow a skirt just so that some dirty old man can lift it up; to have one man rob you of what you have just earned from another; to be at the mercy of the police; to have no future other than a descent into disease and addiction, an institution and an early death. So, you see, you find in me one of the most miserable creatures in the world.'

Listening to what Felicita was telling Babe, Martin could not help crowing, 'You see! I'm half way to winning my bet.'

The man, whose name was Herr Nelke, had stopped off in the bar for an aperitif, so Babe took the opportunity to say to Felicita, 'What I do not understand is how relaxed and happy you seemed when I first noticed you. You were behaving as if you were really fond of Herr Nelke. You truly did look as happy as by your own account you are miserable.'

'Ah well,' sighed Felicita, 'that goes with the job. Yesterday I was robbed and abused by a policeman, today

I have to smile and be happy for a teacher – that's the way it goes.'

Babe had heard enough: clearly Martin was right. They had a good meal and by the end of it were relaxed and talking companionably together.

'Well sir,' said Babe to his guest, 'you seem to have fallen on your feet in this world. Here you are, looking the picture of health, able to afford a pretty girl; you give every appearance of being a contented man. The teaching profession really seems to suit you.'

'Damn teaching!' said Herr Nelke. 'I'd like to send every teacher to the bottom of the sea. I've been tempted I don't know how many times to set fire to the school and to run away and to join the Foreign Legion. I studied Classics at university and did really well, but then found that with my qualifications teaching in a private boarding school was the only reasonably well-paid job available to me. I live in so, between my salary and having my board and lodging provided, I'm pretty well-off financially. But the atmosphere in the school! It's all jealousy and anger and dispute. I escape when I can and spend the money on drink and loose women, but when I get back to my room I feel like banging my head on the wall. Most of my colleagues and the boys also seem to feel the same.'

Martin turned to Babe with his habitual sneer. 'So, have I won the bet comprehensively, or have I not?' On parting, Babe slipped Felicita a couple of thousand euros.

'That way at least she'll be happy for a time,' he told Martin.

'Don't you believe it,' came the reply. 'In the long run you'll just have made her more unhappy than ever.'

'Well, that's as may be,' said Babe. 'But one thing cheers me up: perhaps meeting up with Felicita again is a sign that I'm going to find Madonna-Jo.'

'I sincerely wish that one day she might turn up and

make you happy, but I have to say I think it highly unlikely.'

'You are a hard man,' declared Babe.

'The result of experience,' said Martin.

Babe persisted. 'But just look at those young people sitting over coffee at the tables of that Costa Star. Do they not have the appearance of being utterly contented?'

'You don't see them at home coping with nagging partners and screaming children,' said Martin. 'The rich man squirrelling away his money in the bank they work in has his troubles, the bank clerks have theirs. Maybe the one is a bit better off, but the difference in happiness is so minimal as to be meaningless.'

'The media are always on about a certain Signor Pococuranti, with his fine mansion in the suburb of Küsnacht and his grand receptions,' mused Babe. 'The gossip columns say he is a man who has never had a care in his life.'

'I'd like to see such a rare specimen,' said Martin.

Babe immediately set about procuring an invitation to Signor Pococuranti's.

25

*A visit to the mansion of Signor Pococuranti,
a rich man.*

Babe and Martin took a taxi out to Küsnacht to reach the
mansion of the super-rich Signor Pococuranti. They found
extensive gardens decorated with stone and metal carved
and welded into the most incredible shapes. The mansion
itself dated from the eighteenth century, and its external
aspect though imposing was unremarkable. The master of
the house, sixty or so years old and still looking very sleek,
received them politely but coolly, which rather disconcerted
Babe but was most agreeable to Martin.

They were served cocktails, expertly shaken by two
pretty young girls, members of the Signor's staff. Babe
could not stop himself praising their beauty, their manners
and their skill.

'They're good girls,' said Signor Pococuranti complacently.
'I take them to bed sometimes when I'm feeling sick of the
ladies I meet at parties and receptions, with all their petty
jealousies, their lack of wit or intellectual conversation,
their vanity – and when I tire of all the name-dropping one
needs to perform in order to lay them. But, to tell the
truth, I find I'm beginning to tire of the two girls as well.'

Before dinner they were entertained by a highly
regarded young pianist who played a couple of his own
compositions. Babe was very impressed by the intriguing
rhythms and harmonies.

'It's all right in small doses,' opined Signor Pococuranti, 'but I can't stand too much of it. It becomes very tiring to listen to, though I'm not supposed to say that. It's all about trying to surprise the listener by making a virtue out of ugly sounds: intriguing perhaps for five minutes, but soon becoming boring and offensive. Classical music is no better really: a few beautiful melodies one is supposed to swoon over; a few diminuendos and crescendos where one is expected to rave about the exquisite musicianship of the performer; alternatively, there are pieces of inordinate length which demand monstrous numbers of players so as to impress the public by the sheer cost of mounting the exercise. I've given up attending operas and orchestral concerts, let alone having them performed here.'

Babe tried to put up some kind of defence of music, but Martin was entirely on the Signor's side.

Over dinner they embarked upon a discussion of literature, having reached the dining-room via the library which contained literally thousands of volumes. Babe wanted to know whether Signor Pococuranti could possibly be as dismissive of the great works of literature as he was of classical music.

'My tutor taught me that one of the glories of the English public school education, which has produced so many of our rulers, was the effect on the boys of their reading Homer's *Iliad*,' he said.

'It bores me,' replied his host. 'That continual sequence of battles all sounding the same, those gods who are always interfering but never decisively, the character of Helen who is the lynch-pin of the plot but whom we practically never meet, the city that's besieged endlessly but not captured – it's all so tedious. I've asked other people about it at university receptions and the like: they all admit they nodded off trying to read it, but assert that it is 'a magnificent monument to the glories of the past'. Huh!'

'But,' Babe persisted, 'think of the influence of the Greek and Latin classics on the great European writers who came later. Milton and his *Paradise Lost*, for example.'

'Oh that!' sneered Signor Pococuranti. 'That's just ten books of turgid verse making up a lengthy exegesis of the first chapter of *Genesis*. It is disgusting in its equating of death and sin; it's obscure, it's weird, and the attitude to life it proposes is obnoxious. That's what I think and I don't care whether others agree or not.'

'Perhaps you prefer more modern commentators on the world?' asked Babe rather desperately.

'You are thinking, I suppose, of those myriad winners of all the various prizes for new books. I have them all delivered here, but I've never read one that was of any real quality. Either they rabbit on about the so-called interior lives of deeply boring people – the kind I make strenuous efforts to avoid in the flesh – or they show off all the research they or their employee have done on *Wikipedia* or wherever, padding out their work with long articles of doubtful accuracy on subjects tenuously connected with their plot, utterly confusing in the reader's mind the boundary between reality and fantasy.'

Their excellent dinner over, their host offered them a tour of his palace, which they knew was famed for its display of the art he had collected.

'I have some paintings by the so-called Old Masters – Raphael and such,' said their arts-patron host, 'but only because you can't really not, can you? The truth is they look horribly faded and tawdry, the figures are poorly drawn, the background poorly painted: they claim to depict real life, but actually come nowhere near to it. These paintings by Hockney perhaps come closer to a version of reality, but they are so childish!'

'What on earth is this rather lovely object?' asked Babe,

pointing to what appeared to be the skeleton of a fish encrusted all over with pearls.

'Oh, I bought that because it was the most expensive so-called work of art I had ever had the opportunity to acquire,' replied Signor Pococuranti. 'It is quite pretty, but you are supposed to read a justification of it several pages long in order to understand it as a work of art – something to do with isolating the essence of the sea. I can't be bothered. I collect all these things, but I never look at them.'

Seeing them off from the top of the steps Signor Pococuranti sighed and remarked that he was going to have to have the garden dug up and re-laid as it really was just too boring at the moment. Babe and Martin thanked him politely for a most enjoyable evening and took their leave.

'Well,' said Babe as they walked back down the (to their eyes) delightful driveway, 'there you are. You must agree that we have met here a thoroughly contented man, because he is able to look down on all his possessions.'

'But can't you see,' was Martin's response 'that, on the contrary, all his possessions merely disgust and sicken him? As Plato said a long time ago, the best palates are not those that reject all the food they are offered.'

'But is there not pleasure to be had,' Babe responded, 'in being critically observant and seeing faults that other men overlook?'

'Are you saying ,' Martin riposted, 'that there is pleasure in finding no pleasure?'

'Oh dear!' sighed Babe. 'I suppose there is only one truly happy man, and that will be me when I see Madonna-Jo again.'

'It is never a bad thing to cling on to hope,' said Martin.

However, the days stretched into weeks with still no sign

of Wayne, and Babe was in such depths of despair that it didn't even occur to him that Felicita and Herr Nelke had never sought him out to thank him.

26

*About an evening which Babe and Martin spent
with six strangers, and who they were.*

Babe succumbed to a deep depression. Seriously concerned
about his friend's health, Martin persuaded him that
Zurich was too gloomy a place for someone suffering from
depression. It would soon be Carnival time in Venice: he
should leave a contact number, just in case Wayne turned
up looking for him, and spend a period taking his mind off
his troubles amongst all the distractions that Venice could
provide. Babe agreed – but the journey was to no avail. No
entertainment, nothing Venice had to offer could excite
him, no pretty girl caused him the slightest temptation.

Eventually, Martin spoke frankly. 'You were rather
gullible, to be honest, to imagine that a low-born
adventurer with a fortune already in his pockets would
take it upon himself to seek out your attractive girlfriend
and bring her all the way to Zurich. If he finds her, she'll
become *his* girlfriend. If he doesn't find her easily, he'll
shack up with someone else. My advice to you is forget all
about your pal Wayne and your girlfriend Madonna-Jo.'

Martin's words failed to console Babe who sank ever
deeper into depression, but his friend did not relent,
insisting that this was a world devoid of goodness or
happiness, except, he would perhaps allow, in Eldorado,
which no-one could get to anyway.

One evening Babe and Martin were invited to join six

guests newly arrived at the hotel for a special Carnival dinner. They were about to sit down when Babe's arm was seized from behind and a voice whispered in his ear, 'Be ready to leave with us, don't let me down.'

Turning round, whom did he see but Wayne, hardly recognisable, with a face burnt to the colour of charcoal. Nothing could have surprised and delighted Babe more, other of course, than to have found himself face to face with Madonna-Jo. He went berserk with joy, embracing and even kissing his dear friend.

'If you are here, Madonna-Jo must be too. Where is she? Take me to her so that I can die of joy in her arms.'

'Madonna-Jo is not here,' replied Wayne. 'She is in Karachi.'

'Oh good heavens! Karachi! But were she at the South Pole I would go to her. Come on, let's go!'

'We'll leave at the end of the evening,' insisted Wayne. 'Don't ask me to explain any more now. I'm a prisoner and to all intents and purposes a slave: I have to do as my master tells me. Stay quiet. Have the dinner and be prepared when I give the word.'

Babe was torn between delight and dismay, thrilled to meet up with his faithful friend, amazed at the idea of his being some kind of prisoner, obsessed by the thought of seeing Madonna-Jo again, his heart thumping, his brain bewildered. He sat down next to Martin, who seemed unsurprised by the turn of events, and the six new arrivals.

Wayne poured some wine for one of the men and was heard to say quietly in his ear: 'Sir, the plane is ready. You can go at any time.' So saying, he left the room. As the others looked at each other in surprised silence another of them was approached by one of his staff and told: 'Sir, the car and escort are ready when you are.' The man gestured and the factotum left the room. The guests again exchanged glances of even greater surprise.

A third guest was approached by one of his staff: 'Sir, you should not stay much longer; I'll have everything ready for you to leave.' He too then went out.

Babe and Martin felt sure that this must be part of some Carnival prank, especially when similar messages were given to guests four and five.

But then the sixth man received a different message: 'Mate, they are refusing to grant you safe passage and we cannot persuade them otherwise. It's every man for himself. Goodbye and good luck.'

All the staff having taken themselves off, Babe and Martin remained looking at each other with puzzled expressions. It was Babe who finally broke the silence.

'Well, sirs, if this is all a joke, it's a most peculiar one. Are you not the rich tourists you purport to be? I assure you, Martin and I are no more than we seem.'

Wayne's boss took it upon himself to reply, saying gravely, 'I assure you I am no joke. My name is Gaddaffi. For many years I helped my father rule Libya. I caused the deaths of thousands of my enemies, then escaped death myself only by first hiding in a dung-heap, then trekking hundreds of miles by camel across the desert. I am seeing out my days a virtual prisoner in hiding in Pakistan, although I can access enough of my former wealth in Swiss bank accounts to allow myself the occasional cautious journey, which is how I come to be here.'

The young man next to Mr Gaddaffi spoke next saying: 'My name is Assad. My uncle is President of Syria, but he had to send my mother and me abroad for our own safety. We live a restricted life for our own protection, and any holiday such as this one is a major undertaking and a minimal pleasure.'

The third visitor then spoke up: 'My name is Hussain. When my grandfather was deposed and killed I fled to Rome disguised as a Christian and sought asylum in the

Vatican. I have lived there ever since under the protection of the Pope: today I have slipped away without the knowledge of my guards to enjoy a short holiday at the Venice Carnival. I am risking death, both from any Westerners who might give me up to the Americans for trial and execution, and from all Muslims who could kill me outright for spurning Islam.'

The fourth man said that he was a former member of the Chechen government, forced from his country and hunted by the Russians. The fifth had been a wealthy and powerful archbishop in an African country, which he declined to name, but had been forced into exile for being too liberal.

The sixth man then spoke, 'Gentlemen, I have never enjoyed the power you all seem to have exercised. I was a mere currency trader in a Singapore bank. I coined money hand over fist and lost it just as readily. I made a fortune for myself and lost ten fortunes for my bank and its customers. I am here to enjoy the Carnival with money I haven't got. Tomorrow I have no choice but to throw myself into the Grand Canal.'

The other five listened compassionately and between them offered to pay for his meal. But Babe, to their great surprise – and suspicion – made him a present of a small diamond, enough to see him through the next few months. As they were leaving, four exiled heads of state were arriving to enjoy the Carnival, but Babe took no notice of them. The only thing on his mind was getting to Karachi to find his beloved Madonna-Jo.

27

Babe's journey to Karachi and his arrival there.

Babe's true friend Wayne had managed to procure seats for them on the plane taking Mr Gaddaffi out of Venice.

In the taxi to the airport Babe remarked to Martin, 'Well, I looked forward to having dinner with six VIPs and ended up giving charity to one of them. Perhaps even the rich and powerful can be unlucky. All that's happened to me is that I've lost a few shopping trolleys, but here I am flying to Madonna-Jo's side. Perhaps Fabio was right; perhaps the world is a wonderful place.'

'Maybe,' said Martin.

'But,' continued Babe, 'who would have believed how things turned out in Venice: having dinner with family members of several heads of state, every one of them deposed or disgraced and all coming together in that one hotel.'

'Huh,' retorted Martin, 'that's no more extraordinary than a lot of the things that have happened to us. The overthrow of heads of state is quite a common occurrence. They come nowhere on the 'A' list of celebrities.'

On board the plane Wayne had managed to wangle seats next to him for Babe and Martin, Mr Gaddaffi being of course in the first-class area.

Babe could not wait to quiz his friend. 'So, what is Madonna-Jo up to? Is she still as beautiful as ever? Does she still love me? Is she well? Have you helped her buy a suitably fine mansion?'

'Mate,' sighed Wayne, 'I have to tell you Madonna-Jo is working as a washerwoman for an impoverished ex-maharajah who has very few clothes to wash. I'm afraid the really sad thing is that she has lost her good looks. To be honest, she has grown ugly, which is why Mr Gaddaffi dumped her on this ex-maharajah.'

'Beautiful or ugly,' said Babe, 'I am an honest man and my duty is to go on loving her. But what happened to the fortune you took to her? How has it come to this?'

'Well,' said Wayne, 'I had to give a lot to Don Fernando d'Ibarao y Figuera y Mascarenso y Lampourdos y Souza to get Madonna-Jo away from him. Then, in trying to get out of South America and across to Europe, we fell into the hands of various underworld organisations – the Mafia, drugs cartels, terrorist cells, al-Qaeda, Mr Gaddaffi – who between them cleared us out of every cent. We ended up penniless, stateless, completely in their hands and obliged to serve them effectively as their slaves.'

'What a horrific turn of events!' exclaimed Babe. 'But never mind. I've still got a few diamonds left. I'll soon purchase Madonna-Jo's freedom. It's just a pity she's grown so ugly.'

Then he turned to Martin. 'So, who do you feel most sorry for now: Mr Gaddaffi, Mr Hussain, or me?'

'I really can't say,' was Martin's response. 'To decide that I'd have to be able to see into all your minds.'

'If only Fabio was here,' said Babe. 'He'd be sure to know the truth of the situation.'

'I have no idea in what scales he would feel able to weigh accurately men's misery,' said Martin. 'All I can say is that I'm sure there are millions of people in the world for whom I should feel more sorry than for any of the three of you.'

'You may be right,' said Babe.

They arrived in Karachi and Babe set about negotiations

to ransom Wayne, which he was able to achieve at considerable cost. Without further ado he, Martin and Wayne hired two cycle-rickshaws between them to go slowly along the Sindh river looking out for Madonna-Jo doing her washing. As the rickshaws toiled through the traffic Babe found something strangely familiar about the back of the head of the emaciated man struggling to keep the bike moving. They came to a slope which was more than the poor man could manage to pedal up. He dismounted to push and Babe was able to look him fully in the face. The resemblance was to his old teacher Fabio.

'Do you know,' said Babe to Wayne, 'if I hadn't seen Fabio drowned I could easily believe that it's him pushing this rickshaw.'

'What! Did I hear my name? Is that my Babe?' stammered the man.

'Good grief!' expostulated the driver of the other rickshaw.

'Am I dreaming?' cried Babe. 'Am I awake? Am I really in a rickshaw? That one looks like Sir Harry Thunder-Smith whom I stabbed to death. And can this be Fabio Lamode, my old tutor whom I saw drown?'

'It is, it is us!' they exclaimed in unison.

'You're really telling me this is the teacher whose wisdom I've heard so much about?' said Martin.

They turned the rickshaws round and returned like the wind downhill back into Karachi. Babe explained to the boss who his prisoners were and asked how much it would cost to buy their freedom.

'Well,' said the al-Qaeda man thoughtfully fingering his Kalashnikov, 'if these Christian sons of the American devil are of such note in the West as aristocrats and educationalists, I shall want a hundred thousand dollars.'

'Give me ten minutes,' said Babe.

'Each,' added the boss, and recommended a dealer,

promising to phone him to facilitate the transaction. The dealer did help by giving him two hundred thousand dollars for jewels worth four hundred thousand, and Babe returned happily to pay the money over.

Babe, Sir Harry and Fabio fell to a great deal of mutual hugging and exclamations of delight.

'But how is it that I didn't kill you, my dear Sir Harry? And Fabio, how is it that you are still alive when I saw you drowned? And how do you both come to be pedalling rickshaws on the streets of Karachi?'

'Is it really true that my sister is here somewhere?' asked Sir Harry.

'Oh yes,' said Wayne .

'I've really found my Babe again!' said Fabio.

Babe performed the introductions to Martin and they all went on talking at once. Fabio threw himself upon Babe and thanked him incontinently for paying his ransom. Sir Harry Thunder-Smith nodded his thanks at Babe and promised to repay him the money at the first opportunity. 'And my sister really is here in Pakistan?' he said again.

'Indeed she is. She's a washerwoman for a minor maharajah.'

More jewels were disposed of, a proper taxi was whistled up, and they all set off to find Madonna-Jo and purchase her freedom.

28

What happened next to Babe, Sir Harry Thunder-Smith, Fabio, Martin etc.

'I do beg your forgiveness, Colonel,' said Babe to Sir Harry Thunder-Smith, 'for stabbing you in the chest.'

'Let's forget about that,' said the former colonel and priest. 'I came on a bit strong, I guess. Anyway, to explain how I came to be pedalling this rickshaw, I should tell you that I was taken to the local Catholic hospital where I recovered from my wound. But then I was captured and taken to Buonaventura, arriving in prison there shortly after my sister had left the town. I demanded to be sent back to Rome, but instead found myself posted as chaplain to a UN base in Iraq. I'd barely been there a week when I came across a very good-looking and friendly Iraqi soldier on the base. It being extremely hot and the young man announcing his intention to go for a swim, I conceived it to be my pastoral duty to accompany him. It turned out that for a Christian to be caught swimming naked with a Muslim was a crime of the highest order. I was summarily dismissed from my post and disowned by the UN and, thus cast adrift, found myself in no time in the hands of that section of the al-Qaeda organisation responsible for dealing with hostages from whom there was little expectation of profit. I ended up here being made to work for my small ration of food. But will someone please tell me how my sister comes to be working as a washerwoman?'

'And you,' said Babe, 'my dear friend and teacher, how is it that I find you still alive?'

'So, I was taken out of the interrogation cell and the medic who was supposed simply to go through the motions of attempting resuscitation apparently got a bit carried away and was successful. Having shown my death live on national TV, they had to hush up my recovery, and I was smuggled out in a Forces plane to Afghanistan and put to work in the canteen on the base there. One of my Afghan co-workers befriended me and offered to take me to a private club where his sister worked so that I could experience something of real Afghan culture. His sister turned out to be an extraordinarily pretty and kindly girl and we danced together for some time. She got rather hot and tired and I took her off to a private room where she could take some of her clothes off and cool down a bit, but a group of men from the local mosque burst in and berated us: me as a Christian pig and her as a Muslim whore. She was dragged off screaming in one direction, I was battered and dragged off in the other, first to some kind of cell in the grounds of the mosque, then to be handed over to the same al-Qaeda group as Sir Harry; and so we both ended up as you found us.'

'Well then, my dear Fabio,' said Babe, 'now that you've been interrogated, drowned, beaten, half-starved and forced to labour pedalling a cycle-rickshaw, do you still think that progress has brought mankind to the brink of perfection?'

'I have not changed what I believe,' declared Fabio. 'At the end of the day, I am a sophisticated person and as such I accept that correct ideas are not always susceptible of simple, clear-cut proofs.'

29

How Babe found Madonna-Jo and her companion.

Whilst Babe, Sir Harry, Fabio, Martin and Wayne were telling each other all their adventures, whilst they were debating the significance of all the good and bad things they had seen, whilst they were musing on progress and the lack of it, bemoaning or admiring the rate at which humanity seemed to be evolving towards perfection, they were creeping at something less than walking pace through the traffic, had emerged from the city, and were now in sight of the dilapidated palace belonging to the former maharajah. On the river bank they spotted two washerwomen who turned out to be Madonna-Jo and the old lady.

Sir Harry Thunder-Smith blenched at the sight. Babe, that besotted lover, took in Madonna-Jo's parched skin, her reddened eyes, her flaccid bosom, her wrinkled cheeks, her blistered arms; he staggered back in horror, then out of courtesy advanced to greet her. She embraced Babe and her brother; they embraced the old lady; without further ado Babe was able to purchase their freedom.

Tiffany drew attention to an empty smallholding a little further on into the countryside, and suggested they all establish themselves there whilst they considered how best to move on to a more prosperous future. Madonna-Jo, who appeared not to realise the extent to which she had lost her looks, wasted no time in reminding Babe of the promises he had made, and her tone left him feeling he had no option but to keep his word. Accordingly, he indicated to Sir Harry Thunder-Smith that he would be marrying his sister.

'I shall never accept,' said the son of the baronet, 'that she should marry beneath her, and if you persist I shall be obliged to give you up to the authorities. Somehow Madonna-Jo and I will be going back to England and resuming our rightful place in society. You seem to have found yours, my plebeian friend.'

Madonna-Jo burst into tears, but to no avail.

'You're mad,' cried Babe. 'I've ransomed you and your sister; she has become an ugly washerwoman yet still I'm kind enough to offer to make her my wife, and yet you threaten me with consequences if I do. I'm angry enough to be tempted to kill you all over again.'

'Kill me again if you must,' responded Sir Harry, 'and marry my sister over my dead body!'

30

Conclusion.

Babe had, if he was absolutely honest, not the slightest wish to marry Madonna-Jo, but her brother's opposition stiffened his resolve to go through with it; plus Madonna-Jo was so insistent he felt he had no choice. He consulted Fabio, Martin and his faithful friend Wayne. Fabio gave a well-reasoned speech, in which he demonstrated that a brother has no say whatsoever in whom his sister marries, and that under European human rights legislation the two could marry without recourse to law. Martin suggested throwing the brother into the sea. Wayne's advice was that they should employ their contacts in al-Qaeda to have him ushered willingly or unwillingly in the direction of Rome and the tender mercies of the Father–General of his Order. This course of action was welcomed by the men and approved of by the old lady; the sister was not consulted. The deed was done, at minimal expense, and everyone felt he had got what he deserved.

After so many hardships, thus it was that Babe found himself married to his living-after-all girlfriend and enjoying the company of Fabio, Martin, Wayne and Tiffany. One might perhaps have expected that, with the help of all the wealth brought from the land of the descendants of the Incas, he would be leading a very agreeable existence. In truth though, so many people had been milking him of this wealth that all his remaining store of gold and diamonds had gone into the purchase of the smallholding. His wife grew daily more ugly, more bitter, more shrewish, more unbearable; her companion's health was deteriorating and her temper was becoming even worse than Madonna-Jo's; Wayne did his best in his down-to-earth way, but wore himself out working to support the others, and was for ever moaning about how hard life was; Fabio was in despair at being so far removed from high society and at the lack of internet access without which he could not keep up to date with the march of progress; as for Martin, in his conviction that nothing better could be expected anyway or anywhere, he plodded on patiently. Sometimes Babe, Martin and Fabio would find time for metaphysical debate. On the river and on the road they saw pass by in both directions boat- and bus-loads of refugees and militia fleeing from or going to this or that conflict. These sights stimulated their discussions, but when they couldn't find anything to argue about they were overwhelmed by ennui. On one occasion the old lady was moved to say, 'I wonder which is really worse: on the one hand being raped umpteen times by pirates, having one buttock cut off, being whipped and electrocuted and drowned and beaten, being held captive under conditions of slavery – in short, undergoing all the torments we have been through – or on the other being stuck here with nothing to do?'

'It's a moot point,' said Babe.

Then something happened which served to confirm Martin in his pessimism and to shake the optimistic faith of even Fabio, never mind Babe. Who should turn up one day at the smallholding but Herr Nelke and Felicita, both in a condition of the most extreme poverty. They'd run through the money Babe had given them, had parted, got back together again, then got into difficulties and found themselves for a time in prison. Released, the gentleman had turned to begging and Felicita to her old profession, but neither could make any worthwhile money.

'I did predict,' Martin reminded Babe, 'that your charity would be quickly spent and that they would end up more miserable than ever. You and Wayne between you have gone through goodness knows how many millions of pounds, and you are no happier than Felicita and Herr Nelke.'

'Well, well,' said Fabio to Felicita. 'So there you are, my poor child. Do you know what damage you inflicted on me? And look at you now! Oh, what a world this is!'

This new development caused a further outbreak of debate amongst them.

The elderly Imam of a mosque a few miles away had a reputation for being a particularly wise and open-minded counsellor. They begged audience of him, and asked what it was that so hindered the progress of mankind that the ills of the world seemed no less or different now from what they had been two or three hundred years ago – say at the time when Voltaire was writing *Candide*.

'What would the hindrance be other than that so many have been deceived into ignoring the teachings of the Prophet, peace be upon him?' replied the sage.

'But,' objected Fabio, 'the Islamic world we see around us shows no signs of being any better than the Christian world we came from.'

'Get out of here!' roared the Imam. 'Get out, before I have you stoned to death!'

As they left the mosque some of the locals shook their fists at them and hurled insults.

'They can't have heard already about what you said,' said Babe to Fabio.

It turned out that the Norwegian Consul in Karachi had been murdered and the West was threatening reprisals. They managed to leave the town unscathed, and on their way back to the smallholding an old man smiled benignly at them from his chair placed under the orange trees outside his front door, where he was evidently enjoying the evening freshness. Fabio, always eager to investigate other peoples' views, stopped to ask him if he understood why the Norwegian Consul had been shot.

'I have no idea,' replied the old boy. 'I know nothing of what goes on in Karachi. It seems to me that those who involve themselves in politics and public affairs end up meeting miserable fates which they probably deserve. So I never take any interest in what the media tell me is going on in the big cities of the world. I just tend my little patch of land and make shift to sell what I produce.'

So saying he invited them into his house. His two sons and two daughters were at home and helped him serve the strangers a magnificent feast consisting entirely of home-grown produce. In addition to the wonderful food and drink they also appreciated the delicate aromas which made their visit a delight.

'You must have a pretty large farm to produce all this,' Babe said to the old man.

'Only twenty acres,' was the reply. 'My children help me tend it. The hard work keeps at bay the worst ills, namely boredom, debauchery and hunger. We are content.'

As they continued on their way home Babe's head was full of what they had just seen and heard.

'You know,' he said, 'it seems to me that that old man was far better off than any of the dignitaries we had dinner with in Zurich.'

'Being a top man does have its dangers,' said Fabio. 'Think of Julius Caesar, King Harold, Richard II, Edward II, Richard III, Anne Boleyn, Louis XVI, Napoleon, Mussolini, Hitler, Kennedy, not to mention Hussain, Gaddaffi and co. If you think about it …'

'What I think,' said Babe, 'is that we need to make it our business to tend our piece of land.'

'I'm sure you are right,' said Fabio. 'We should align ourselves with the workers of the world.'

Every member of the little group entered into the spirit of the enterprise, each according to his or her own talents. Their little plot of land became very productive. Madonna-Jo, though she remained ugly, became an excellent baker and pastry-maker; Felicita and the old lady took superb care of the clothing, making and mending for them all; even Herr Nelke turned out to be first-class at DIY, and turned into an honest man into the bargain.

Sometimes Fabio would say to Babe: 'You know, it is all a question of progress: sometimes we regress in order to progress. Things went backwards when you received the late Sir Digby Thunder-Smith's shoe in your backside, when you were under interrogation, when you had to trek across South America, when you knifed the young master, when you lost your wealth-laden shopping trolleys; but as a result you have progressed to living bountifully off plentiful fruits and vegetables.'

'Very true,' Babe would reply, 'but now let's stop theorising and get back to producing.'